I0579680

Lone Hearts

A LINES IN THE SAND NOVEL

HOT TREE PUBLISHING

Lone Hearts © 2020 by Lindsay Detwiler

All rights reserved. No part of this book may be used or reproduced in any written, electronic, recorded, or photocopied format without the express permission from the author or publisher as allowed under the terms and conditions with which it was purchased or as strictly permitted by applicable copyright law. Any unauthorized distribution, circulation or use of this text may be a direct infringement of the author's rights, and those responsible may be liable in law accordingly. Thank you for respecting the work of this author.

Lone Hearts is a work of fiction. All names, characters, events and places found therein are either from the author's imagination or used fictitiously. Any similarity to persons alive or dead, actual events, locations, or organizations is entirely coincidental and not intended by the author.

For information, contact the publisher, Hot Tree Publishing.

www.hottreepublishing.com

Editing: Hot Tree Editing

Cover Designer: BookSmith Design

E-book ISBN: 978-1-922359-13-1

Paperback ISBN: 978-1-922359-14-8

Lines in the Sand Series

Inked Hearts

Wild Hearts

Promised Hearts

Texan Hearts

Hidden Hearts (MM)

Lone Hearts

Stand-Alone Romances

Remember When

Still Us

The Trail to You

Who We Were

To Say Goodbye

All of You

Then Comes Love Series

Then Comes Love

Where Love Went

Where Love Went: Holiday Special

To my husband

ONE

Cash

——————

SHE ROLLS OFF ME, BITING HER LIP IN THAT COME-hither way, my body still reveling in the sweet release as she sidles up to me underneath the sheets. Between the lingering effects of our sex and the buzz from the alcohol, I know for sure only one thing: This has got to be what heaven is like.

I groan, rolling onto my side as she snuggles up to me, the warmth of her breasts against my back making me wonder if I could go another round.

"Do you want me to stay?" she whispers in the seductive voice I've come to recognize but not love. At this exact moment, Killer kicks the bedroom door, whining and scratching. He snaps me to my senses because I almost said yes.

Dogs are truly a man's best friend.

"Early morning tomorrow. New case. Sorry, Casey. Maybe next time." I cuddle into the pillow and feel her exhale, her breath slapping against my back.

"Fine," she says, and I can sense the tension in her words. It's nothing new. This is the dance we've been playing for the past two months, this dangerous but sexy game of passion and walls.

I should feel bad, but the fact is—I'm a dick. I don't feel one ounce of remorse. She's known from the beginning what this was—sex. Nothing more, nothing less. Hot sex between two consenting adults.

The problem is, no matter how much Casey denies it, I think she's convinced she can pull the sweet, settled side of Cash Creed out of me. I think the business suits I wear by day, the lawyer face, and the professional confidence send her the message that I'm a man waiting to settle down. In her mind, she's probably got us married off and living in the white house down the street from my parents, two kids in the front yard and Killer, my Jack Russell, traded in for a Lab. Two lawyers raising the perfect lawyerly family in the middle of the perfectly quaint town.

The thought, although perhaps endearing, makes me want to gag. No freaking thanks. I've seen enough divorce cases come across my desk to know that love just doesn't work out. But sex, well, sex always does.

Almost always.

"Goodnight," I murmur, sitting up to watch her slink back into her clothes. "I'll call you?"

"Yeah, Cash. I'm sure you will," she mumbles as she rushes out the bedroom door to let herself out of my apartment. I sigh. I feel a little bit like an asshole. Just a little bit. Plus, if word gets out at the office and Mama and Daddy hear how my professional relationship with one of their best attorneys isn't exactly professional anymore—yep, my ass is toast.

I might be a bit of a player and I might be twenty-six, but I'm a Texan boy through and through. I'm smart enough to know my mama can still kick my grown ass. I still sneak my sexual escapades around like I'm in the FBI. Woodville isn't exactly population a million. It's hard enough to keep a girlfriend secret in this place, let alone nightly romps with all the lawyers and professionals in town.

What can I say? I have refined taste in women. And that refined taste just so happens to lead me to many of the women in our office. Not quite ethical or smart, perhaps. But thinking with my brain instead of—well, other things—has never been my strength.

I lie back on my bed, Killer now jumping up with me. I think about kicking him down, the smell of sex and tension still palpable. He licks his paws, turns three circles, and plops down by my feet. I decide to let him stay. Hands behind my head, I stare up at the ceiling, thinking about basically nothing. Feeling basically nothing.

What the fuck is wrong with me? What kind of an animal am I, acting like some frat boy? Maybe Mama and Daddy are right. Maybe it's time to start thinking about settling down.

But then I think about what that means. I think about the wild and reckless Levi, my brother, who has "settled down" despite all denials of it. Sure, he's got a gorgeous girlfriend, and he seems pretty happy. Nevertheless, when I think of who he used to be and what kind of fun he used to have, I can't help but feel a little bit bad for him. So much of him is lost, even if he won't admit it, and that's just not something I want.

I have a good life. It might be a little bit of a rambling man who's stuck in one small-town kind of life. It's a life where I spend Saturday night sexing it up with a hot blonde and then sleeping it off with my dog licking his feet at the bottom of the bed. It's the kind of life where I go to Mama's on Sundays just so I can get some home-cooked food. It's the kind of life where I'm surrounded by people but always a little bit alone.

It's probably the booze talking, I reassure myself. I'm always a bit of a depressed drunk. I turn back onto my side, closing my eyes and deciding to drift off. I can leave the psychobabble bullshit for another night. I'm wiped. And I really do have to be at the firm early tomorrow to finish up a discovery. Probably should get around to sleeping it off. Mom and Dad will be furious if they think I'm coming to work hungover. Of course, I'm basically a pro at hiding it at this point. What the hell else is the single life in your twenties for if it isn't for partying and having a blast?

I close my eyes, reassuring myself that I'm doing it all right, when my phone buzzes. I think about ignoring it, but then it keeps buzzing. Maybe it's Casey. She probably forgot her key or something.

Shit.

I sit up, slapping the nightstand for the phone until I find it, unhooking it from its charger and unlocking the screen. By the time I swipe, the phone's stopped buzzing. I glance at the screen and recognize the number on the missed call screen.

It's Levi. Something tells me he's not just calling to see what I'm up to.

"Hello?" I ask after redialing his number.

"Cash, it's me. Man, I don't know how to tell you this. It's not good." Levi's voice is strained. My heart stops. I've never heard him like this.

"What is it?" I ask, hating the waiting. I want to know right now what it is. I hate this delay.

"It's Grandpa."

"Is he okay?" I ask, my initial thought confirmed.

"Cash, he's dead."

I inhale deeply, processing the information.

"Shit," I say, not quite the comforting words I'm sure Levi was looking for.

"Yeah. It's just.... God, it's awful."

"What happened?" I ask after clearing my throat, running my free hand through my hair.

"Heart attack. Cindy found him in the shower. It was too late when they got there."

I can hear Levi choking up, trying his best to sound strong through his sadness. Levi was always close to Grandpa, so I know this has to be hard.

"I'm sorry, bro," I say, meaning it.

"Can you please go tell Mom and Dad? I don't want to do it over the phone. I think one of us should be there."

I stand up, scratching my stomach as I head for the light switch.

"I'm on it right now," I assure him.

"Are you drunk?" Levi asks.

"Maybe."

"Then make sure—"

"I call an Uber. I know, brother. I'm not a moron." Despite the situation, I roll my eyes at my brother's continual insistence on treating me like a child.

"Well, Cash, no offense, but sometimes for being a lawyer...."

"I'm not very mature. I know, I know. I've got it covered. I'll call you in the morning, okay?" I say. I should be annoyed. As the baby of the family, everyone treats me like an idiot.

But I can't think about that now. As I dig out some clothes and search the Uber app for a driver, all I can think about is Grandpa and how, in the flash of a moment, everything in life can change.

In the flash of a moment, everything in life can seem just so upside down, sex and booze aside.

TWO

Cash

————

THE NEXT FEW DAYS ARE A BLUR AS THEY SO OFTEN ARE
at crucial crossroads in life. Plans are made at the firm
for my parents and me to head out to Ocean City,
Maryland, for a few days. Grandpa didn't want a traditional funeral, which isn't surprising to those who
knew him. He wanted his ashes to be scattered at sea
—from the speedboat in the middle of the ocean off
Ocean City, to be exact. Yeah, Grandpa always had a
flair for the flashy. Aunt Pearl and Uncle Alvin aren't
up for the long trip, so Molly Madigan's parents—
Levi's old flame—are going to stay with them.

God bless them. I left a few bottles of vodka
behind. They're going to need it, especially since Aunt
Pearl thinks Mr. Madigan is pretty okay—her words—

in the looks department and was already hitting on him.

After boarding the plane—Killer's along for the ride too, since I've kind of grown attached to the guy—I settle into my seat, finally breathing for the first time in days. Mom and Dad sit beside me, Mom especially a mess. This week hasn't been easy on the family, to say the least. I think we're all in shock. Staring out the window, I watch as Texas sinks away, the clouds surrounding the plane.

Although I'm not happy about the circumstances, a tiny part of me is a little excited to be getting away from this sleepy town for a few days. I know Levi's been loving Ocean City. It'll be interesting to see my big brother and to find out what all the fuss is about. There are also the practicalities—there are a lot of legalities to tend to with Grandpa's business and will. I lean back in my seat, closing my eyes and trying to rest up for what's probably going to be an even more intense few days.

"THIS JUST FEELS... DISRESPECTFUL," MOM SAYS through tears as she clutches her soggy tissue.

"Mom, it's what he wanted," Levi argues as we stand at the loading dock, Levi holding the urn, Jodie by his side.

We're getting ready to board The Rocket, the speedboat Grandpa specified in his funeral wishes. The June sun beating down on us, we stand in all black—which, in hindsight, wasn't the best idea. I wipe some sweat from my head as I help Mom onto the boat, Dad following closely behind. Cindy's mascara's running down her face as Levi and Jodie help her onto the boat as well. I shake my head a little at the sky.

Grandpa, you've sure got one hell of a way of going out, I think to myself. I have to give him credit. It's definitely not your traditional, mopey service. I think when I go out one day, I'd like nothing more than to be scattered to the wind from a speedboat.

Some of Levi's new friends who knew Grandpa are also along for the ride. We've already had all the introductions—Avery, Jesse, Phoebe, Lysander, Reed, and a few of Grandpa's stuffy business associates who look horrified about getting on this thing. I have to admit—I'm kind of excited to see how fast it goes.

"Better not cry," I whisper to Levi as I take a seat beside him.

"Little brother, you're the one we're worried about," he replies, shaking his head.

"Five bucks Dad pukes," I say, outstretching a hand.

Never one to turn down a competition, my brother shakes my hand. "Make it ten."

And with that, the boat takes off—and I do mean takes off. There's no time to worry about sadness or final goodbyes. The pastor who gave a short prayer service at Midsummer Nights this morning—Mama insisted there would be some sort of traditional, spiritual goodbye despite Grandpa's wishes—is turning green. I let out a "yeehaw," and some of the others on the boat follow suit.

The wind is whipping in my face, and it feels like we're soaring on the water. It's a thrill, and even though it's under horrible circumstances, I can't help but smile at the sight of our family on this crazy boat, Mama's wild hair even wilder on here, and Daddy clutching the seat for dear life. Maybe Grandpa knew what he was doing. Maybe he wanted to scare us shit-less, so we didn't have time to be sad. When we get to the middle of the ocean, the boat idles as we prepare for our final goodbye.

"We love you, Grandpa. Thanks for reminding us

all to live fearlessly," Levi says, before opening the urn. He tosses a handful of ashes into the water before passing the urn to Cindy.

"I love you forever," she whispers to the wind, and even though I'm a man who doesn't really believe in love, I feel a pang of sorrow for her. Her heart is clearly cracked. This is a defining moment in her life —she'll never be the same. Another reason not to let love get the best of you, in my opinion, but to each his or her own. The urn passes hand to hand as everyone says one final goodbye, Grandpa drifting out to sea, freed from all the chaos and calamity of this life.

When we've all tossed Grandpa to the sea and Mama complains one more time about the unconventional ceremony—I remind her that these were Grandpa's final wishes and it would be disrespectful to not follow them—the boat heads back, and Levi and I spend the rest of the ride studying Dad to see who is going to win the bet.

We're getting to the dock and I'm starting to worry I'm going to have to cough up some cash. But just as we're nearing the dock, Dad starts to look green. Like really green. And before we pull in, he's puking up his breakfast waffles all over Mama's shoes. This makes Mama cry even harder. The boat pulls into the dock, the boat operator looking horrified at the mess as everyone rushes to help Mama out. Lysander and Reed, two of Levi's new friends, assure her they can get her a suitable pair of shoes in a jiffy while everyone else comforts her.

"What, am I chopped liver? Anyone worried about me?" Dad asks in true Ray Creed fashion, hands in the air as everyone rushes off.

"No way. You're my hero right now. Thanks to you, Levi here owes me some money. But I'll take payment in the form of a drink at the bar during the luncheon," I say as Levi shakes his head.

"You *would* want a drink at a funeral luncheon," Levi says, rolling his eyes.

We walk down the dock as Dad comes between us putting a hand on each of our shoulders. "Nothing much that can't be solved with a little whiskey, boys."

I nod, smiling at the sentiment I've heard dozens of times over the years.

"You're lucky Mama's so worried about her shoes that she didn't hear you," Levi says.

"Truth. But what your Mama doesn't know can't really hurt her, right? Now come on. While she's busy getting new shoes, how about you buy your dad a good strong drink too. After that crazy ceremony, I think we could all use a little escapism, and something tells me wherever he is, your grandpa, God rest his soul, would be cheering us on."

"I think you're right," I reply, knowing wherever Grandpa is, he's smiling at the chaos he's created—and probably laughing a little too.

SITTING AT THE BAR AS SOME OF GRANDPA'S FAVORITE songs blare through Midsummer Nights, the bar and restaurant that Levi's friends own and hang out at, I throw back another shot, trying to shove aside all the feelings of loss.

"I'm gonna miss him," Levi says, taking a stool beside me as Jodie, his girlfriend, follows.

I turn and grin at my big brother. "Remember that one time he took us fishing?"

"Oh, I remember," Levi says, smiling. "How many did you drink that day?"

"Four?" I ask, thinking of the memory.

"How old were you?" Jodie asks.

I smirk. "Fourteen."

"Levi and Cash Creed, you rebels," she says, and Levi and I raise our beers in toast.

"Grandpa knew how to be a little bit rebellious," Levi says, and I agree.

"What are you boys talking about?" Mama asks, sneaking up behind us. Her face is still tearstained, but she's not sobbing anymore. She's wearing some pink water shoes Reed managed to scrounge up at a boardwalk shop nearby.

"Nothing much," I say, knowing some things are better kept secret, especially from Mama.

"I'm sure," she says, plopping down on a bar stool by us.

The rest of the crew wanders over, Lysander ambling behind the bar to serve up some more drinks.

"Thanks for letting us have the luncheon here," Mama says, and Lysander nods.

"Least we could do. So, how long are you guys staying in town?"

"Just until things are in order," Mama answers.

"Well, you know, it is prime tourist season," Reed announces, joining Lysander behind the bar to help out. He looks at me. "A handsome man like you might find it interesting to stick around during peak season." He winks at me, and I grin.

"Peak season in Texas is all the time," I reply, and Mama hits my arm.

"Reed's sort of right, you know," Jodie adds now. "All the pretty young things will be coming right in. You never know what opportunity might come up.

And I know someone who could find you a rental pretty cheap," she says, looking at Levi.

"Speaking of rentals and business," I say, "Is ten okay to go over the business details of the will tomorrow?"

I'd taken the reins on the will, knowing Mama and Dad had their own things to worry about. Figured it was the least I could do. It should be pretty straightforward. Grandpa was a little crazy sometimes, but he also liked to keep things in order.

"Yeah," Levi says. "Better go tell Cindy." He gets up from the stool, leaving Jodie and me with an empty stool between us.

"I'm glad you're all here," Jodie says to me, a soft grin. "I mean, I know the circumstances aren't great, but I'm glad Levi has family around now. It's going to be hard without his grandpa here."

I take another drink of my beer before responding. "I know Levi and Grandpa were close. Not that I wasn't, but these past couple years, Grandpa and Levi have obviously grown closer. I'm glad he has you, though, to lean on."

And I mean it. I haven't seen Levi happier, even when he was with that gorgeous Molly Madigan. I was always pretty jealous growing up that he got the beautiful girl across the street, although after the whole rodeo accident when she showed her true colors, I knew perhaps I'd just been spared.

Still, seeing Levi with Jodie, it makes me smile to see how my rebel brother's definitely been tamed. It's working for him, and I couldn't be happier, if it's what he really wants.

I also couldn't be happier it's not me—I've still got plenty of freedom, plenty of women to explore, and plenty of fun to have. While he's shopping for curtains and quote pillows, I'm stocking up on booze and good times. I think I've clearly got the better gig going.

"She's pretty great," Avery says now, sidling up to us. "But she's right. It's good to have family close for this. Your grandpa was a good man, even though I only met him a few times. He'll be missed."

"Um, I hate to interrupt, but I just want to make sure this is right," Reed says, leaning across the bar from me. "The playlist you gave me has this song on it. Is that correct? I mean, I know your grandpa wasn't traditional, but I didn't want to make anyone upset."

I glance at the last song on the list, smiling. "Oh, that's right. I told you Grandpa taught us our rebel ways."

And so, Reed fires up the jukebox, playing a song that stops Levi dead in his tracks across the restaurant, and we both share in a laugh at the moment Grandpa forever sealed in our memories.

"To a wild man with a rebel but warm heart," I say, lifting my beer, silently saying goodbye again to the man who taught Levi and me to live life fearlessly, recklessly, and with no regrets.

THREE

Cash

———

WE GATHER AT LEVI AND JODIE'S, ALL OF US CROWDING in their living room, including Killer. Their cat, Sebastian, isn't too happy about Killer, and Killer's not too happy about Sebastian. I guess they'll figure it out.

"Now," I say from my position on the sofa, my parents, Levi, and Jodie crowded around. Cindy is also here. I go through a ton of legal jargon and dole out assets. I'm pretty excited that he left me his jet ski, although there's not much I'm going to be able to do with it back in Texas. Cindy's been left with a pretty hefty payout even though they weren't married. Grandpa also left her the condo, so she'll be sitting comfortably. Luckily, my family's not the type to get all crazy over money, so there aren't any protests.

Except when we get to the businesses.

"That's got to be a mistake. Grandpa knew I was running Wild Hearts. This will must be old," Levi says when I announce that Grandpa's rental business in its entirety has been left to Levi.

"He updated this thing just last month. He meant for you to get everything," I say.

"You did talk about helping with the rental business once we got Wild Hearts running," Jodie notes.

"Yeah, but I didn't plan on all of that now. And when we talked about that, I never planned on Wild Hearts growing so much." Levi readjusts the hat on his head, exhaling.

"Son, death doesn't really leave room for plans. You know that. You've got it under control," Daddy says.

Levi shakes his head. "I love Grandpa for leaving me the business, but honestly, I can't handle this right now. Not with Wild Hearts."

My brother's horse-riding ranch just outside of the beach town was a booming attraction now. It kept him and Jodie busy every day of the week. I could sympathize with his worries because Grandpa's rental business was more like an empire at this point.

I look over to Cindy. "Any chance you can help

out?" I ask. I know she and Grandad were close. Maybe she knew enough of the ropes to help out.

"Sorry, I just... I can't. I really can't." Her face is still tearstained like it's been for days. Grandpa and Cindy might have been a fast-burning flame, but there must have been some depth there too because Cindy is just broken up over this.

"I'll help as best as I can," Jodie whispers, stroking Levi's back.

The room is silent for a long moment before Levi looks up, staring at me as I thumb through the will, making sure I didn't miss anything.

"Cash?" he asks.

"Yeah, brother?"

"Why don't you stay and help."

I scoff at the idea, shaking my head like I must've heard him wrong. "What?"

"Stay. Just for a while until I get things situated. I mean, come on. You've got a legal mind and even though I hate to admit it, you're pretty damn smart. Running a business will be child's play for you."

"I wouldn't call it child's play," Daddy adds.

"Still, come on, Cash. Couldn't you use a change of pace? Where's the wild, live-it-up brother you claim to be? Why not do something different, try something new?"

I shake my head. Grief must be really warping Levi's mind if this is a serious offer. "I love you, brother. But you know I'm busy back in Texas. I can't just leave everything behind. And I can't just come up here and run a rental business I know nothing about."

Levi raises an eyebrow. "I know you could do it. I'm sure you could be spared for the summer. And besides, there are plenty of gorgeous things to keep you busy here, too."

I take a deep breath. Levi must've lost his mind. Me? Running a rental business in Ocean City? Sure, I've got a knack for contracts and legalities, but this is a whole different game. "I don't know, Levi. I don't think I'm the guy for the job."

"Oh, don't be silly," Mama adds now. "Cash, you know you've got a great mind. You're charismatic and levelheaded. You could really be an asset for Levi here. And maybe he's right. You could use a change of pace."

"Mama, are you forgetting that I'm your employee?"

"Come on, son. It's summer. There'll be interns pawing at the doors. Your mother's right. Sometimes a change of pace can do a man good." Dad leans back in his chair, arms crossed like the decision has been made.

I stare at Levi, a little wounded by my family's willingness to let me go and replace me so quickly. Still, I think about how it might be nice to get a change of scenery. I don't know much about rental properties and all that, other than the legalities behind the contracts. Still, I do know my way around a bar of scantily clad women, and this town doesn't seem to have a shortage of that. Maybe a fresh set of women to chase, a new town could do me good. If nothing else, it could be fun. It's been a while since I've had a summer vacation of sorts, even if it is a working summer vacation.

And all those bikinis. I tap my foot, leaning back in my chair now.

"Your grandpa would love the idea," Mama adds.

I eye her suspiciously now. "I don't think he would, or he would've left it to me in the will."

Dad laughs. "Son, he knew you. He knew that if he told Cash Creed what to do or even hinted at it, you'd do the opposite. It's who you are."

I take a deep breath. Dad's kind of right. I don't like being told what to do—although they're trying to tell me what to do now.

Nonetheless, I convince myself this is what I want to do, not what I have to do. "Okay," I say, envisioning a summer of tanning sessions gazing at gorgeous, bikini-clad girls.

"Wait, okay as in you'll do it?" Levi asks, leaning forward.

I sigh. "Just for the summer. Don't get any ideas that you're going to convert me to whatever weird beachy religion you follow here that sucked you right in," I warn as Levi stands to come over and hug me.

"Oh, thank heavens. This place worked for one of my boys," Mama says, raising her hands as if in worship.

"Mama, don't go getting any ideas either. Just because Levi settled down—no offense, Jodie—doesn't mean I'm going to. Far, far from it."

"We'll just see about that," Mama adds, and for the first time in days, she smiles.

I roll my eyes. I love how my life, my love life, has become a family conspiracy.

"You never know what could happen. Sometimes even the lone hearts get lucky," Ray Creed adds now. Great, even he's on the "get married, Cash" train that Mama's driving.

"That sounds like a really good country song," Jodie adds, smiling. "So Cash, where are you going to stay? We have a spare bedroom if you're interested."

I raise an eyebrow. "Thanks, I appreciate it. But

one, I think Sebastian would jump out the window if Killer stayed here any longer." With that, we look at the growling cat, ears down, who stands with an arched back in the corner of the room, Killer licking his paws in front of the feline. "And two, no offense, but I've heard from Avery, Lysander, and Reed that you two can barely control yourselves in public. I love you, big brother, but not enough to hear your nightly sexcapades through the walls. I think it might cramp my own adventures, if you know what I mean."

"No, Cash, we don't know what you mean. Enlighten us," Mama says, raising an eyebrow as she scowls.

"No worries, Mama. You don't want to know. But anyway, thank you for the offer, Jodie. As landlord of several fine properties now, though, I think I'll be able to find something that suits me."

"There's always the apartments we started in," Jodie says, looking at my brother wistfully.

I shrivel my nose. "Again, no offense. I'm really no snob, but I've seen some of the tenants that come out of there." I gesture toward Levi, grinning. "I think I'll take a peek at these condos off the boardwalk.

"Of course you will," Levi says, rolling his eyes. "You always did like the finer things."

"Nothing wrong with that, brother."

"I suppose," he says, and I tuck the will safely inside the file as I head over to the corner to rescue Sebastian from Killer, thinking about how much life is really going to change—and how I definitely didn't pack enough for this extended stay.

FOUR

Sage

———

"Harper, you're such a bad influence on me," I murmur into the phone that's propped between my ear and shoulder as I pull the steaming cup of coffee off the Keurig. It's my fourth of the day, even though I've been swearing I'll cut back. Tomorrow's another day, though, and I've got a few more hours of marketing reports to sift through.

"No, I'm a good influence. That's why you hired me. First, for my mad design skills. But mostly because I keep you from being freaking boring. Now come on. Those marketing reports aren't going to disappear, and reading them isn't going to change anything right now. Let's go. You're turning into a boring old hermit in that freaking condo of yours."

"Okay, I'll have you know that I went to Target twice yesterday, and I even took a spinning class this morning. I'm not turning into a hermit. A hermit, by definition, never leaves the house."

"Well, in my definition, a hermit never leaves the house to do anything fun. Sage, are you seriously trying to tell me that Target and spinning class are the epitome of your social life right now? Come on. You're freaking twenty-five, you're gorgeous, and you're loaded. You're supposed to be enjoying it. Get out. That's the beauty of working for yourself. You can decide when you get a vacation."

I shake my head as I set my coffee on the end table. Monticello is meowing at his bowl, so I lean down and give his clammy skin a pat before filling up his black dish that says Prince. Barcelona ambles out from behind the television, his safe spot. He sits beside the dish, pawing at his whiskers before leaning down to the bowl as well.

Harper keeps talking about spinsters and crazy cat ladies and other terms I should find offensive, but I don't. I know Harper just worries about me. In truth, she's not completely wrong. I am turning a little boring. Actually, a lot boring.

Of course, there's always work. Work's been a blast lately.

Spoken like a true workaholic, I know. Nevertheless, I've always felt like if you're doing what you love, it's not really work. And I've also always felt like when you get complacent about money and schedules, that's when you fail. Failure is not a word in my vocabulary, never has been—the one positive thing my parents left me with.

"Are you listening to me, or are you petting those cats right now like you always are?"

"Guilty as charged," I say, standing up to walk over to my coffee and the file of reports.

"Well, listen. I'm not taking no for an answer. Boss or not, I'm telling you that you have no choice in this matter. When's the last time you went out to a bar?"

I mentally tick back the weeks. "Probably the beginning of May," I reply.

"You are aware it's June 10 right now, aren't you?"

"And your point?"

"You're losing your touch, Sage Everling."

I glance at the reports, work beckoning me forward. But then I think about the bar scene, about how long it really has been since I've gotten out. It's been my longest dry spell in a while—self-imposed, which makes it even worse.

"You're right." The words roll off my tongue easier than I expected, but I can admit when I'm wrong.

Harper's right. She's good for me. She reminds me what life is about and when I need to loosen up. And I feel the unquenchable need to escape for a while, to relieve some stress in the best way.

"Wait a second," Harper says, and I can imagine her stance, her head flipping as she tosses her two black braids behind her. "Did you just admit I'm right?"

"Yes. You're right. It's been about five weeks since Rocky, and I guess work can wait. A woman has her needs, and I'm feeling like I could go for a good challenge tonight. Plus, it's tourist season. My favorite, and the best time for no-strings-attached fun."

"That's the spirit. So what do you think? Professional type? Artsy? What are you going for?"

I smile as I head to my room to pick out my go-to going out outfit. "You know, Harper Renault, not every woman's best friend is this nonchalant about casual sex. Some best friends actually hope their friend finds a serious relationship."

"Yeah, but I know that's not your gig. Every woman has her own gig, you know?"

"Yes. Besides, your obsession with your one-and-only is enough serious relationship for the both of us. Anytime I want to feel depressingly traditional, I live vicariously through you. You talk about me losing my touch and being boring. I mean, pretty soon you're going to be married with the white picket. Pretty soon *your* weekly excitement will be Target."

"Well, that's why I'm glad I have you, with your eternal prowess. I can live vicariously through you when I become a boring, washed-up housewife. We really do balance each other out beautifully, as friends of course. We'd be terrible lovers."

I shake my head at her comment and at the thought of artsy, overall-wearing Harper being the soccer mom type. It's actually a riot.

"I don't think that's going to happen in this life-time. I'm happy that Brad is making you happy, even if I do think sex with one man for the rest of your life is a tad morose."

"Well, you play love your way, and I'll play mine. But still, player or not, you are being a bit boring lately. Let's get back on the winning streak, what do you say? I'll pick you up in an hour. The Marooned Pirate sound good?"

"Perfect," I reply. I love the loud atmosphere there. I love that few people recognize me in the dim lights.

Not that I'm a famous celebrity or something. Still, when people recognize the CEO of the self-made fashion design empire, they're always asking for free Evermore handbags or scarves or outfits. And I love my fans, I love doing giveaways, but there comes a point when I have to escape work, you know? Plus, I'm not keen on seeing myself on the tabloid papers when there's a slow celebrity news day. The last picture of me and Rocky wasn't very flattering, and I definitely got a lot of backlash online. I like to keep the media focused on my line, on my products, and not on my sometimes-scandalous love life.

"No Brad tonight?" I ask, truly surprised Harper's able to tear herself away from his hip. Since they met at a yoga class seven months ago, Harper's been over-the-top in love.

And I *am* happy for her. It's not that I don't believe in the value of love or monogamy. I just don't quite believe in it for me. After all, I'm modern. I'm independent. I'm happy just the way things are. And sometimes, contrary to popular belief, a woman just doesn't have time for a relationship *and* fun—so I'll take fun, any day of the week. Target, spinning class, or seduction at its finest, whatever the day calls for.

"Not tonight, chica. It's just you and me... and whoever you deem a worthy catch."

"See you soon?"

"You bet. Meet you out front."

I click off the phone, sigh, and shut down my computer.

Sometimes even the biggest workaholics have to get out and play.

FIVE

Sage

———

"SEE? ISN'T THIS MUCH BETTER THAN THOSE DAMN marketing reports?" Harper asks before clinking her margarita against mine. We've claimed our usual table, one I haven't been at for a while.

"It does. You're right, I kind of lost my touch there. I feel a little rusty."

"Well, launching a new line that *Vogue* names the hottest line of the year will do that, you know?" she says, and I shake my head, blushing a little. I've worked hard to rise to the top of my game, but I'm still humbled by the fact it's actually working. Seeing our handbags, our scarves on some of the hottest names in Hollywood these past few months has been ridiculous.

And kept me ridiculously busy.

It's really no excuse, though. I've always been good at balancing work and fun. Tonight will have to be the night I even the scale, balancing out all those long nights these past few months.

"Guess I'll just have to make up for it tonight."

"You might be a little out of touch, off your game. Sure you're ready to play?" she teases as we scan the room.

"You just wait. I haven't lost my touch yet. Oh, and I think Mr. Right for Tonight just walked through the door." I gesture toward the front of the Marooned Pirate, where a crew has just walked in. A blonde and a redheaded girl animatedly chat, both hanging on the arms of some pretty good-looking men who are clearly taken. Another couple, both male, amble in behind them, chatting animatedly as they wave to another group of friends. They're both dressed with an amazing sense of style—hey, even when I'm here for fun, fashion's my thing.

But in the middle of the crazy, loud group who I've seen here a few times before, there stands a man in some nice designer jeans and a button-up shirt. He's clean-shaven, just like I like them, and he's tall, super tall. He screams business professional and maybe even a little bit arrogant from his walk to his stance at the bar. He's scoping the place out, and he glances over at me, staring for a little bit longer than a friendly appraisal. I give him a coy smile as I sip my margarita. He's here to play, and so am I. This might just be the perfect night to catch up on some fun.

"Who is he?" Harper asks.

"I don't know, but I think I'm going to find out."

"Go get him. He's freaking gorgeous. Play nice."

"Don't I always?" I ask, feeling the drink settle into my veins and boost my confidence.

I let down my ponytail strategically, tossing my hair to the side as I walk over as confidently as possible, my stilettos leading the way. The man in blue doesn't take his eyes off me. It feels good.

Some women are uncomfortable with sexuality, with my mindset about love. I get it. It's not for everyone. But for me, sexuality equates to power, something I'm fine with having. I use it wisely and I use it respectfully—two consenting adults and all that. There are no pretenses or manipulative endgames. It's just adult fun, adult sex, and adult needs being met. Nothing more. The rest of the women can have all that mushy stuff. I'm just in it for physical needs.

I amble up to the tall, handsome stranger and say, "Hi, I'm Sage. Can I buy you a drink?" I don't like to tiptoe around it. And the type of guys I like, well, they seem to like forward.

"Cash Creed. And how about we do things the other way around? What are you drinking?"

I smile confidently up at him, his eyes making my heart flutter in a way it hasn't in quite some time. "Mr. Creed, that's not how I do things. I don't need any man to take care of me."

"Is that so?" he asks.

"I can take care of myself. So how about I buy you a drink, you tell me all about yourself, and then you ask me to dance?"

"Forward much?" he asks, teasing me with his eyes. I get a whiff of his cologne, and it's the kind of expensive scent that makes me a little crazy. I'm liking this guy, the sexual chemistry radiating already.

"Always. Life's too short for anything else."

"Jack and Coke then," he says, and I smile, brushing past him to flag down the bartender.

Beside Cash, the redhead and the blonde are whispering, studying me. "Hi, I'm Sage," I say in a friendly, nonthreatening tone. I'm all about playing hard and having fun, but I don't have room for being bitchy. If this guy's taken, I'd rather know now before I get too into things.

"Avery Johannas," the blonde says.

"Jodie Ellison," the redhead announces, offering a small wave and a smile.

"Nice to meet you. Do you mind if I steal this one for a bit?" I ask.

They both shake their heads, grinning.

"Just making sure. Have a good night," I say as I hand Cash his drink and pull him to an empty table nearby.

"So, Cash Creed. Your accent tells me you're not from around here," I note, making small talk, taking this guy in, and mostly making sure he's not a creep. Coming with a group of friends who look respectable and who are regulars is a pretty good sign.

"Nope. From Texas."

"What brings you here?"

"Grandfather's funeral," he replies, his eyes piercing mine.

"Oh, God, I'm sorry," I say, seriously feeling bad. *Wow, way to go Sage. You* are *rusty.*

"It's okay. You couldn't have known." He shrugs, taking a sip of his drink, his eyes still piercing into mine.

"So are you in town for long?" I ask, trying to recover.

"For the summer, actually. I've got some things to help with. How about you?"

"This is home for me."

"Good to know," he says, still studying me. I've met

a lot of guys, but there's something about this one. I can't quite put my finger on it. Part of it is in the way he looks at me when I'm talking. It's like he's drinking me in, those eyes staring but not in a creepy kind of way. In a way that makes me flutter in all the right ways.

He takes a sip of his drink and we endure some more necessary small talk before he finally leads me to the dance floor. "Oh, sorry," he says, when the song switches from a slow song to a fast one just as we're getting ready to dance.

"For what? I'm not much for slow anyway," I reply, smirking as I start dancing wildly to the upbeat song.

Cash joins right in, his body next to mine, the heat from him melding into me. It feels good to connect physically with someone. God, I've forgotten how good it feels. Harper's right. Those marketing reports can wait. In the middle of the song, he smoothly spins me around so I'm facing him, pressing me up against him. This isn't his first rodeo, either. His smooth moves, his swagger tells me he's not a stranger to a life of fun.

"Girlfriend back home?" I ask, studying his eyes. I might be all about no strings attached, but I like to make sure the guys I'm with really don't have any attachments. I have my boundaries.

"No. Boyfriend?"

"No. And if I did, I guess he wasn't really making me happy if I'm here with you like this," I reply.

At this, he leans down and takes my lips with his, hard and fast. The kiss momentarily stuns me because I just wasn't expecting it. It's been a while since I've met a guy who can match me for being forward. Usually, I'm the dominant one in the relationship.

Still, as his lips move expertly on mine, I drink it in, the sounds of the club fading into the background. All I know is that his lips are on mine and it feels freaking amazing, his hands on the small of my back with just the right amount of pressure. His hands wander up the back of my white jacket, a tank top still shielding my skin from his hands.

I've never wanted to lose my shirt so much. I've never cursed myself so much for wearing so many layers.

"Will you get a room, brother? Jesus, we've been in the club for what, twenty minutes, and you're already causing a scene?" another voice with a deep drawl says, snapping me out of it. A man in a cowboy hat stands in the middle of the dance floor now, the redhead on his arm. He looks like he could be Cash's more rugged twin. Must be his brother.

"This is my brother, Levi," Cash confirms. "My

older, bossy, protective brother. Cock block much, bro?"

Levi shakes his head. "Nice to meet you. Be careful with this one," Levi says to me, pointing toward his brother. "He's a little rough with the heart."

"I can handle it, but thanks for the warning," I reply, still shaken from the kiss.

"Come on, killjoy. Cash is a big boy. Let these two have their fun," the redhead says, winking at me. I smile as Cash leans in. "Do you want to take this somewhere else?"

"Forward much?" I ask, raising an eyebrow.

"Some gorgeous woman told me it's the best way," he says. I look back at Harper and give her a quick nod. She's playing on her phone but looks up to see me. I give her the nod, which is our signal that all is well. She gives me a thumbs-up to let me know she's leaving before I follow Cash out of the bar.

"Your place or mine?" he asks.

"Yours," I say. It's one of my unwritten rules. It might be a little riskier, but I'm a girl who likes to live on the edge. And to me, the risk of accidentally misreading a serial killer is less of a risk than letting a guy into my space, my real life. The Sage of the club is part persona, part wall protecting me from others knowing the real Sage Everling. I prefer to keep it that way.

"Well, I just moved in, so there isn't much furniture," he murmurs, pushing a strand of hair out of my face.

"Is there a bed?" I ask.

"Yeah, there's a bed. Although, I must say, I've been told I work my best magic in nontraditional settings."

"You'll just have to prove it to me," I reply, excitement rising as I follow him down the sidewalk toward a night of all kinds of excitement.

SIX

Cash

———

She's beautiful, but her confidence just adds an extra level of perfection for me. I like a woman who knows what she wants and goes after it. Sage doesn't disappoint.

At the door to my condo, I fiddle with the lock, my palms sweaty. Killer barks, trying to sound more ferocious than he is. Once I get the door open, I pick him up so he doesn't nip at my guest. I don't need another cock block tonight.

"Cute dog," she says, reaching out to pet Killer. Before I can warn her about his tendency to snap at strangers, she's petting his head, and he's licking her. Apparently she's managed to win him over already. Of course, he's not the only one she's won over in a short amount of time.

Maybe it's the way her perfectly wavy blonde hair falls over her face just enough to be intriguing. Maybe it's the expensive clothes she wears or the way her hips sway just a little bit as she walks. She knows she's sexy, but she doesn't overdo it. She's mastered the confident, forward vibe I go crazy for. I like a woman who knows what she wants. I like a woman who isn't a "yes" woman. I like a woman who likes power, and I think Sage might just be all that.

And I can't believe how lucky I am that this woman is coming home with me tonight.

I feel a little twinge of guilt as I lead her into my almost-empty condo, a sad, lonely couch and a coffee table the only furniture in the place. I haven't invested too much time in this place because I'm not staying all that long. A bed, a couch, and a decent television—what more does a bachelor need? Looking around now, though, I feel like it's inadequate for a woman like Sage. As I head to the fridge to pull out a bottle of wine I had chilled—I'm nothing if not prepared—I think to myself: is it inadequate? And what is a woman like Sage like?

We've got the chemistry, and I know she's forward. But who is this woman? What does she do for a living? What's her story? And what's her last name?

Snap out of it, Cash, I tell myself. *No use getting all*

sentimental now. It's never bothered me before. Sex, nothing more. It's my thing. And it seems to be Sage's thing too because as I'm pouring wine, she's sauntering up to me, her eyes averted to the floor as she takes off her jacket in a smooth, sexy move.

"So, you did say you have a bed, right?" she asks before biting her pouty, plump lips in a way that makes me crazy.

I raise an eyebrow. "No small talk first? No getting to know me?"

She shrugs. "I only need to know one thing. How are you in bed?" she asks, a hip jutted out.

I grin, shaking my head. "You'll just have to find out, I guess."

"Then what are you waiting for?" she asks, her voice sexy and smoky.

She grabs my hand, and I exhale loudly through my mouth as she leads me back to the hall, me giving her verbal directions as she pulls me to my room. Once inside, she yanks me into her, kissing my mouth hard and fast, her tongue swirling purposefully against mine. Her hands wander to my belt, and I inhale through my teeth, a rush of air filling my lungs as I feel the excitement build.

"Are you sure about this?" I ask.

She raises an eyebrow. "Are you getting all soft on me now?" she asks, winking.

I smile for a moment before pulling her body against mine, letting her know just how not-soft I am. I murmur in her ear, "Not a chance. Just want to make sure you're sure."

In response, she undoes my belt and slides her hand inside my boxers, grabbing me as I slowly kiss her neck. I don't know who this Sage girl is or what her last name is, but I know one thing: she knows how to have a good time, and she's not shy about letting me know it.

I INHALE DEEPLY, THE TENSION RELEASED AND grogginess taking over my body. Sage's arm is against mine, and the feel of our skin together feels good.... Not as good as a few moments ago, but good nonetheless.

I turn to look at her now, her hair stuck to her forehead not making her any less beautiful. Her full lips, her blue eyes—she's the total deal. She's everything I'm sexually attracted to.

For a moment, I stare at her, liking the sight of her in my bed, liking the feel of her beside me so much that I consider what it would be like to fall asleep beside her. I think about what it would be like to let her fall asleep in my arms. I think about breaking my steadfast rule, one I haven't broken in five years—I think about letting her stay.

But then reality sinks in. This isn't some cheesy-ass romance novel. This is a one-night stand about to become a few-hours stand. It was fun, it was wildly fun, but that was it. Asking her to stay will just lead to clingy phone calls and tears and all sorts of things I don't want to deal with. I look to her, ready to tell her I have an early morning and I need her to leave—accompanied by my smooth, charming smile, of course.

"Well, it's been fun, but I have to get going," she says, sitting up abruptly before I can choke out the words.

"Wait, what?" I ask, the words spewing from my mouth.

She looks at me as she wraps up in the comforter, standing to gather her clothes. "Yeah, it's been fun, Cash. But I'm going to go."

She blows me a kiss before heading to the bathroom with her clothes in hand. I hear the door shut, and I stare up at the ceiling.

What the fuck just happened? Did she really just

get up and leave? No asking to stay, or waiting for me to tell her to leave? She just... left? After all that? Was it not enough? Was it not good for her? All of these questions swirl in my mind, panic setting in for a moment.

And then I come to. What an egotistical idiot I'm being. I mean, I was just about to ask her to leave. So what if she left first? I'm being a chauvinistic ass right now. Still, I have to admit—it stings a little. She doesn't want to stay. Is this how I made all those women feel over the years? Shit, I didn't really think about that. Before I have time to psychoanalyze myself anymore —how the hell did this thing get so complicated?—I stand up, heading to the hall in my boxers, feeling like a bit of a weirdo. She emerges from the bathroom a few minutes later, dressed, with her bag on her shoulder.

"So, can I call you or something?" I ask, not filtering my words before they just burst out. This is not routine. I never ask for a girl's number. Again, it's just not in my rules. But seeing her leaving, thinking this could be the last time I see Sage, it doesn't sit right. At all. I don't want this to be goodbye. After sex like that, after chemistry, how can we just say good-bye? Wasn't it at least good enough to do this—whatever this thing is—again?

"Um, no. Sorry, but that's not really my thing," she says, shrugging. "It's not you, it's me. Really. It was fun. Really fun, Cash. Maybe I'll see you around sometime. Thanks," she says, as if I just delivered her a pizza or handed her grocery bags at the supermarket. With that, she marches right out the condo door. Killer doesn't even get up and bark at her, passed out on the couch. The door to my condo clicks shut, and I stand like a moron in the doorway to my bedroom for a long moment in my boxers.

And just like that, Sage is gone, and I'm left behind asking: what the hell just happened?

SEVEN

Cash

———

"OH, HE'S HERE. THANK GOD. CASH CREED, YOU BETTER be dishing about how your night with Sage Everling was. Did she show you any of her upcoming designs?"

I stare at Reed like he's speaking a foreign language as I take a seat at a corner booth. Jodie and Levi, who are at Midsummer Nights for breakfast, rush over to join me. Lysander also crowds over.

"Don't you all have a business to run or something? Or a couple of businesses?"

"Oh please, the morning rush hasn't started. And hearing all about your night is way more important," Reed replies. "Now spill. Details?"

"How do you know her last name?" I ask, the thought striking me. I'm not quite a morning person, and I'm dying for some coffee. But I'm guessing I might as well get all this out of the way first or I'm never going to get that coffee.

"Are you kidding me right now?" Reed asks, looking at Lysander and shaking his head like I've just committed a felony. I shrug.

"Oh my God, I swear. Do you people live in a bomb shelter or something down in Texas? Sage Everling, you know, founder and CEO of Evermore?"

I look to Levi, still shrugging. He does the same.

"Is that supposed to mean something to me?" I ask again.

"Oh, man. You're lucky you're out of hitting range," Lysander chimes in. "Evermore is only Reed's favorite design line."

"Those new bags they released last month are gorgeous, and the clothing line is edgy with sophistication. They're supposed to be releasing a men's line in a few months, and I'm dying to get my hands on some pieces. When I saw you with that woman last night, I was fanboying, but Lysander wouldn't let me come and interrupt."

"Because I know how you get. And I figured Cash deserved some fun."

"You didn't stop Levi and Jodie from wandering over," Reed argues.

"They don't fanboy over designers like you do."

"Wait, can everyone just slow down," I argue. "So you're telling me the woman I slept with last night is Sage Everling, the self-made millionaire I've heard so many women rave about? Like, she makes those fancy handbags and all that? Are you serious?"

I had no idea. I mean, now that I think about it, Sage has the confidence you need to be a self-made millionaire. She clearly goes after what she wants without mercy. But still, I didn't realize I was with basically royalty.

"So you slept with her! I knew it. You owe me ten bucks," Reed says now, looking at Lysander. "That woman had her eye on you from the second you walked in."

"You're just hoping there's a wedding so you can get free groomsmen gifts from her," Jodie adds now, rolling her eyes.

"You slept with her? Jesus, Cash, you've only been in town a few days, and you're sleeping with the area's wealthiest, most influential woman? Good thing Mama already went home because I'm sure people will be talking about this one... and if she finds out her precious, do-no-wrong angel is wrapped in the sheets with Sage Everling, wow is she going to be pissed."

"It kind of disturbs me that your family still

pretends you two are so righteous," Jodie says now, wrapping an arm around Levi.

"They're both charismatic smooth talkers. Which is how this one snagged Sage Everling. So did you go to her place? Tell me what the décor was like. I bet it was to die for," Reed continues, practically squealing.

"We went to my place," I say. "Now, can I get some coffee, please, since you're all interrogating me? Jesus, you'd think a grown man could have an ounce of privacy about his sex life."

"Apparently you don't know how this group of friends works," Jodie answers. "Nothing is sacred or private, especially not sex lives."

I shake my head as Levi and Jodie talk about Reed and Lysander's meddling in their relationship before it was a relationship, but I only half hear them. I'm thinking about the woman from last night.

She's freaking gorgeous, confident, and successful. She's the real deal. Then again, this complicates things. Maybe this explains her whole leaving game from last night. A woman like that has to be careful because I'm sure so many guys are just after one thing —her money. Which I could care less about. I mean, let's be real, I'm not a lawyer for free. I earn decent paychecks, and I can appreciate the finer things in life. But for me, my "relationships" are about lust and that's it. I don't expect anything out of them other than a night of fun.

So why then is this woman still plaguing my mind? Why did I wake up this morning in a funk over the fact she left without a single care? Why did hearing her name, her full name, send a jolt right through me?

"So really, what was she like, bro? She seemed a little forward if you ask me," Levi says, snapping me back to it as Reed slides a coffee to me. I warm my hands on the mug, thinking about it, coming to the realization I didn't want to come to.

"Well, I think I may have met my match," I say.

Reed claps, wedding bells probably ringing in his ears. I look at him. "Not that kind of match. I mean, I met my match in the game."

"Wait, you mean the player met a formidable opponent?" Levi asks, chuckling as Jodie squints at me questioningly.

"I mean," I say, shaking my head as I think about her walking out last night, "the ultimate player may have just gotten played."

"Wow," Levi says. "You're losing your touch."

I sigh, staring out the nearby window at the board-walk, thinking that maybe I deserve this a little bit. You can't play forever and not get burned. Still, as I watch a couple stroll down the boardwalk, hand in hand on this cloudy Tuesday, I think about how it isn't the whole getting played aspect that bothers me. No, if I'm being honest, the part that truly bothers me is the fact that for some reason, it seems like she's different. I can't get those damn eyes, that sensuous voice out of my head.

And I don't like it one bit.

"Little brother, I think you may be in trouble in so many more ways than one," Levi says as Lysander walks over with the newspaper.

I look at the headline in shock, staring at a dusky photograph from the Marooned Pirate. In it, Sage is grinding on me.

Players Gotta Play: Sage Everling's Newest Score.

"Oh shit," I say, feeling like a complete moron.

Yep, it's true. I've finally met my match.

I TRY TO SHOVE THE SAGE EVERLING DILEMMA OUT OF my mind as Levi takes me to the apartment complex to scope out the situation. It's been a hectic week with the absence of Grandpa really settling in. Besides the emotional grief, there's also the practical side of things. Luckily, Levi learned the ropes about the rental business. Still, he's so busy with Wild Hearts, and I don't have much experience as a landlord. Running the condos plus the apartments plus dealing with the other rental properties is going to be a lot to handle.

"Dear God, is that really a pink flamingo on the front lawn?" I ask as we pull up to the apartment complex Levi and Jodie used to call home. Phoebe, Jodie's mom, apparently lives in the double apartment downstairs although I haven't seen much of her. Maybe it'll be a good thing, though, having some friendly ears and eyes in the complex.

"Brings back memories just walking in this place," Levi says, grinning as he opens the office door and leads us inside.

"Still hard to believe he's gone," I say, thinking about Grandpa as I see his nameplate on his simple desk in the office.

"I miss him like crazy. Life's so short, huh?"

"Yeah. It is. But I guess that's why you've got to get your kicks in now."

Levi smiles. "Grandpa would agree with that."

I take a seat on the wheelie desk chair, leaning back as Levi sorts through some paperwork on the desk. I stare up at the ceiling, sighing.

"What is it?" Levi asks. "Don't tell me you're still freaking about your 'tarnished' reputation in the paper. I mean, you'd have to have a reputation, a good one, to tarnish it."

I scowl at my big brother before shaking my head. "It actually isn't that, but thanks for reminding me that I was played and everyone knows it."

"Kind of karma and all that, you know?" he says, flipping through some paperwork.

I stand, walking over to the window that looks out over the ocean, thinking about how nice it would be to just go fall asleep on the beach instead of dealing with all of this—Grandpa, the business, Sage. But that's so like me, shutting down when the emotional baggage gets hard.

"I just feel bad, you know?" I say, confessing it aloud for the first time. Levi stops rustling the papers and ambles over beside me, looking out the window as well. "I wish I'd have visited him before he died. I just got so wrapped up in my life back home, I didn't even think about it. I didn't think about him. I mean, we were so close when we were young and then—"

"Hey, Cash, don't beat yourself up. It's not like he lived a block away, you know? And you might not have been here for Grandpa, but you were there for Mama and Daddy when I wasn't. We've both made sacrifices, and we've both paid our family dues in our own way." He pats me on the back. "Now stop stalling. You've got a lot to learn. If you ever want to get back to that club and have fun again, you've got to get all of this mastered."

"No worries. I'm a fast learner."

Levi walks me through some of the basic paperwork and must-knows before taking me on a tour of the apartment complex. I'm listening to advice I'm never going to remember about water heaters, electric, and all kinds of things I didn't really think would fall under my realm of duties as he walks me out to the front of the building. Standing on the lawn, taking in the sight of the somewhat sad-looking apartment complex, I notice a door opens on the far right.

Out pops a scantily clad woman, tan and dark haired. She's got her long, wavy locks tossed loosely in a bun, her huge aviator sunglasses shielding her eyes. Still, her body's tight in all the right places, those shorts she's wearing barely covering enough to be legal. Her tank top hugs her as I study her. She notices, giving me a smile and a little wave. I nod and wave back.

Levi kicks me. "You've got work to do. Don't get distracted."

"Since when did you turn into a killjoy? Let a man have his fun, you know?" I reply as I ignore Levi and walk over toward the gorgeous woman.

"Hey," I offer casually, hands in pockets so I don't look too desperate.

"Hi. Are you the new landlord?" she asks, shoving the aviators back on her head to reveal green eyes that sparkle in the sunlight.

"I sure am. Cash Creed," I announce, extending my hand to shake hers, mostly just because I want to see what it feels like to have her hand in mine. It feels damn good, her perfectly manicured hands lightly grasping mine.

"Nice to meet you. I don't think I've ever seen you around."

"I'm from Texas. I moved up after my grandad died."

"I'm so sorry. I've only been here a few months, but he was such a nice man. Well, listen, I know what it's like to be new in town, so if you need someone to show you the ropes, just let me know. I'll give you my card." She hands me a pink business card that says Layla Goodman, Personal Stylist. Her number is at the bottom.

"I'll definitely take you up on this," I say, holding the card up as she winks and then walks away, heading toward the beach.

"You know, I don't think running this place will be so bad," I say, smiling as I watch her leave.

"Haven't you learned your lesson after yesterday's debacle?" Levi asks. I hold up the card.

"I have. Go for the woman who isn't afraid to tell you her name. And if you get played, the best thing you can do is just get back on the horse and all that."

Levi rolls his eyes. "How do women stand you? Seriously."

"It's my Texan charm."

"That's my line," Levi replies.

"Well, last I checked, you don't need that line anymore because you've got yourself a woman."

"You've got that right. Now come on, we've got some more people to meet if you're going to run this place this summer."

"Isn't it time for lunch?"

"Jesus, Cash, do you do any work back home? We've only been 'working' for an hour."

"Well, brother, if you worked the family business like the rest of us, you'd know there are some perks to it. But all right, kill my fun. It doesn't matter. I've got her card, so I can catch up with her anytime I like."

"Can you at least maintain some semblance of a professional appearance while acting as landlord? I don't need you pissing off all the female renters."

I follow him out of the building as we head for the next stop. I tuck the card in my wallet, thinking about how beautiful Layla Goodman is and how much I'd love for her to show me around town.

This is exactly what I need. A good time, just like at home, without any strings attached to forget all about that Sage Everling and her games.

EIGHT

Sage

"There's no hiding your fun from last night," Harper says as she hands me a cup of coffee and the newspaper. I graciously accept the cup of coffee as I glance at the paper.

"You've got to be kidding me," I whine, staring at a fuzzy picture of myself in that white blazer from last night, Cash right behind me.

"Oh, come on. You know you're a celeb in this town. No use fighting it. What's the big deal? It's not like you're married or something."

I toss the paper on my desk, groaning. This is the last thing I needed.

"You know what the big deal is. I don't need clients and everyone else thinking I'm some joke just because I like to have fun. I like to keep that personal. And up until yesterday, my good times at the Marooned Pirate were just that. How the hell did this happen?"

Harper shrugged. "You're getting more famous. That's how. I think it's a good thing. No publicity is a bad thing and all that," she says, plopping down on my sofa.

My office area is actually just a desk by the bay window in my living room. I like to feel comfortable in my space, and I like to be able to look out the window at the ocean. The benefits of the view and all that.

"I know, but I don't want people talking. My personal life and how I live it really shouldn't be what the press focuses on."

I sigh. Last time I made the paper like this a few months ago, the comments on social media were not really about my work. They were more about what some thought of my "loose" love life. I haven't missed being in the press for that.

"Honey, it comes with the territory. Even if you were married with the two children expected, people would complain. It's part of the role, you know?"

"I know. But I don't want it to take away from my work, from our work. We've got this men's collection launching in a couple months. I don't want some guy I met at a bar to be all anyone talks about when they think of Sage Everling and Evermore."

I stand from my desk, shoving aside the marketing reports once again, thrown off by this. I know Harper meant well by keeping me in the loop, but sometimes I prefer to stay oblivious.

"So, speaking of this guy at the bar, tell me. How was it? How was he?"

I smile, turning to look at her. "I mean, didn't I just say we've got a new launch coming soon? Shouldn't my lead designer be, I don't know, working on some of those final touches?"

Harper waves me off. "Relax, boss. You know I've got this."

"Oh, I do."

"Then humor me. Take off the boss hat you wear so well and put on the friend hat."

I grin as Barcelona ambles up, rubbing my leg. I pick him up, plopping on the seat by Harper. It's true. I hired Harper Renault a few years back because I was impressed by her work. But now, I'm thankful I hired her because of so much more than her fashion sense. She's become my best friend, my only friend really. She gets my workaholic nature, but she also helps me keep it under control. And she doesn't judge my love choices too much.

"Okay, well, he was pretty great. We had obvious chemistry. It was a fun time."

She raises an eyebrow. "A fun time? That was it? That man oozed chemistry, but he also was so much more than that. I don't know, you two just looked good together, and you seemed to jive."

"We did jive. It was fun. But it was a one-night thing." Harper grins.

"What?" I ask, a little annoyed as Barcelona walks over to her.

"Nothing. It's just... that grin. I don't know. Seems like Cash Creed really got to you."

I shake my head. "Yeah, okay, so it was a lot of fun. But you know my rules."

"Which are super stupid, by the way. What's so wrong about falling for someone? What's so wrong about more than one night?"

"You know the answer to that," I say, sighing as I lean back, looking at the ceiling. Harper's been my friend for long enough now to know my reservations. I have a lot of them.

"There's such a thing as a prenup."

"Not for dating. And besides, it's not about the money. You know that's not it."

"I know. But I think you sell yourself short. Is it so crazy to think a man would fall in love with you, Sage? You're beautiful and smart, but you're also fun and loving. You've got all these amazing characteristics. I think it's sort of a cop-out that you just assume a man would only be with you for your money."

I shake my head. "Well, if the past has taught me anything—"

"Okay, so there are some assholes out there. But trust me, they're not all assholes."

"Well, Cash Creed had enough swagger to tell me he's probably one of them."

"And how do you know this?" she asks.

"I don't know. He just seemed too cocky."

"Because he had sex with you? Um, double standards much?"

"Okay, fair enough. But I don't know."

"You're right. You don't know. You were with him one night. But he didn't seem so bad from the little I saw of him. He actually seems like he could be a good match for you. And I've looked him up. He's from a family of lawyers back in Texas. Seems pretty legit. And that brother of his runs Wild Hearts, so there's some business sense in the family."

"Well, it doesn't matter. I'm not going to see him again."

"I hope you do. I think you should give him a chance."

"Please. No thanks. That's not how I operate. Business and work first. Love is a side dish, you know?"

"Sage Everling, I love you, but you're a jerk when it comes to love. If I was a lesbian, I'd marry you just so you could see that long-term commitment isn't the enemy. Don't you ever want to just, I don't know, share all of this amazing life with someone? Don't you get lonely?"

"I don't have time to get lonely," I say, but even as I'm spewing out the words, I know their validity isn't sold.

"You're not fooling anyone, least of all yourself."

I exhale. "I've got marketing reports to get back to. Are you going to work on designs here or your usual spot?" I ask, dodging the statement like I do so well. Work's always been there for me, especially when I don't feel like dealing with the emotions of something.

"I'm heading to my spot. Want to come with? It's half-price latte day."

"No, I think I'll stay here and get my work done. Love you," I say, meaning it. Even when Harper's shoving some not-so-easy truths in my face, I know she means well.

"Love you back. Now get to work. Geez, am I the only one around here who cares about your business?" she teases as I shake my head and walk her to the door.

"Let me know when you've got the finishing touches completed," I say.

"And let me know when you decide to give Cash Creed another try," she mutters before waving and shutting the door.

I lean against the door as Monticello meows at my feet. I look down, smiling at him. "Of course, we're not lonely, right buddy?"

Even the cat looks at me like I'm nothing but a lie.

NINE

Cash

———

It's a few days after the Sage Everling sexcapade when I decide to head out in public—other than for work.

Okay, in truth, I'm not really feeling like I need to hide. So I was spotted with one of the hottest, most famous women in Ocean City... is that such a bad thing? If anything, I think it enhances my reputation. But then again, maybe it's just a cover for the fact I'm still a little shocked.

The player isn't supposed to get played. That's just not how it's supposed to work. More than that, the player isn't supposed to still be thinking about the beautiful woman days later, wondering what she's doing, wondering if I'll see her again. Dammit, that woman is good.

Killer's barking at the end of his leash startles me back to real life. Sitting on the bench with Killer glued to my side, I glance around at the other dogs and their owners having a blast in the leash-free park. Killer's the only one on a leash—but he's also the only dog who doesn't appear to be very dog-friendly. Looks like bringing him here was yet another dumb choice on my part. I thought maybe the socialization and fresh air would be good for him, for both of us. Guess this wasn't the case.

I sit on the bench, trying to rein Killer back in, scolding him for his snarling at a fluffy golden retriever that strolls by us. Walking him is a sort of hippie-like girl, black braids down her back. She's wearing quite an interesting outfit, neon yellow and hot pink mixing in a way that isn't unattractive—it's just very loud.

"Sorry," I mutter as she stops to stare at Killer, smiling.

"No worries. I've had a few who thought they were bigger than they actually were. Dogs I mean," she says, chuckling.

"I see," I reply, shaking my head as she stoops down to see Killer. "He's a bit nippy," I warn, but she's already patting him on the head. He quiets, seeming to take in the sight of the girl. Maybe she's a dog whisperer because Killer actually seems to like her. That makes two women in the past few days. Weird.

"I've got the magic touch. Dogs love me," she says, matter-of-factly as her golden retriever dashes off to play with a great Dane. "So what's his name?"

"Killer," I reply.

"An apt choice," she says, smirking, studying me. "Did you pick it or your girlfriend?"

I grin at her attempt at being sly. "I did. No girlfriend in the picture, not that you were asking, right?"

"No, of course not. Just... wondering is all."

She sits beside me on the bench, a little closer than I would've expected. I don't get the sense she's flirting though. It's like she's got some sort of a mission, but I don't know what. I don't know anyone in this town, and I don't know this woman, that's for sure.

"So have you lived here long?" she asks.

"So do you interrogate everyone at the dog park?" I ask, sort of in a joking tone but also in a way that says I'm serious.

"Maybe. I'm sorry. I'm a little inquisitive sometimes. I just... I like to figure people out, you know?"

"I see that. But no, I haven't lived here long. Just moved here, actually. I'm just here for the summer."

"Oh, here to party, or here to work?"

"Work mostly. Party, too. I like to have fun."

"Interesting," she says, grinning. "I know someone else like that."

"Oh?" I ask, now scanning the dog park to see if there's some shy, embarrassed woman around. I'm wondering if this woman was sent over to scope me out.

"Yeah. She's this odd concoction of workaholic meets party girl. It works for her, but not so much in the love life department. It's hard for her to find someone who understands, who is able to look past her nonchalant attitude toward love. I think deep down she's waiting for someone to understand, for someone to push her out of that weird state of limbo. If only she could find the right someone, the right guy to keep up with her but also to challenge her a bit, you know?"

"Sounds like an amazing woman."

"She is. If someone just would take the time to get past her 'I'm only having fun' exterior. But that's all something for another day. Cute dog, Cash. Thanks for letting me see him." She hands me Killer as she starts to walk away.

I stare at her ambling over to reclaim her dog, wondering why our conversation felt so... staged. So weird. And then it hits me.

She knew my name, but I never mentioned it. I

never mentioned my name. How the hell did she know me? And is every woman in this town operating under a hidden agenda? I stand, carrying Killer as I head back home, my mind trying to wrap itself around the dating situation here. I thought Ocean City was going to be prime real estate for having unregulated fun, crazy one-night stands, and a rocking good time. Now, I'm starting to realize that maybe all Ocean City's going to give me is a bunch of enigmatic situations with women I can't even begin to unravel. For the first time in weeks, I'm homesick for the uncomplicated, unrivaled fun back home.

TEN

Cash

"Cash? Hello? It's me, Jodie. Listen, you need to get to Midsummer Nights right now. Like, right now. She's here."

I groan, my head trying to process the female voice, trying to push through the grogginess to piece together the meaning of the statement.

I roll over in bed, the phone still to my ear. "Who? Who is where?" I ask.

"Cash, get it together. That woman you were with, Sage. She's here for breakfast at Midsummer Nights. Lysander and Reed told me to call you. This could be your chance."

I take a deep breath, sitting up and running my free hand through my hair. "Chance for what?"

"A chance to talk to her again, to see her. Come on,

Cash. We all know you were crazy about her. You can feed that player crap to Levi, but we all see it. You're into her. So get your ass over here and talk to her again."

I stagger out of bed, last night's drinks still weighing heavily on my body. I glance in the mirror. I'm a wreck. If I'm going anywhere, I need to get myself together.

"Okay," I say, mostly to placate the woman on the other end of the phone, but also because I really don't know what to say.

Do I want to see Sage Everling again? And what will I say?

This isn't like me. One and done, even if it sounds prickish—which it unarguably is—that's it. I don't pursue women. I don't chase them down for another night of fun, and if I do, it's only because I know they're only in it for one thing. I don't ever risk them thinking I'm in it for a relationship. But as I slap on some cologne and toss on some jeans, I think about how this feels different. Uncomfortably different.

Because as I head to Midsummer Nights, I'm thinking about all the right things to say and wondering what she'll be wearing. I'm wondering if I could snag another date with the current queen of fashion design, and if I do, where we'll go. I'm thinking not like Cash Creed, the ultimate lone heart. I'm thinking like Cash Creed, a man falling for a woman he barely knows.

"Shit," I mutter to myself. This is going to be an epic disaster, and I'm going to head back to Texas with my tail between my legs, wishing I'd just stayed home. Love never brings anything good, I've learned, and lonely hearts are better off. But this damn woman has me forgetting rational and forgetting sexual. She's got me thinking like a man in love—and I hate every second of it.

Still, despite my brain screaming at me to turn around and let it go, I find myself sauntering through Midsummer Night's doorway within fifteen minutes of Jodie's call, the bells ringing to announce the presence of a soon-to-be broken man.

"Oh my goodness, look who it is," Lysander announces loudly from the register as the woman he's talking to turns.

And when she turns, shooting a look at me from those icy blue eyes, I mutter, "Shit" again.

Because when I see her in front of me in the middle of the day, I know without a doubt the fluttering in my chest isn't a heart attack—heart attacks can be treated, but this disastrous thing can't.

"Hey," I mumble, the usually suave words that

aimlessly fly out of my mouth choking up in my throat. I shove my hands in my pockets, trying to play it cool, trying not to show her how much those tight black pants and hot pink blouse are getting to me.

"Hi," she says, offering a weak smile.

"Oh, look, seems like your card is working after all, Ms. Everling. Sorry for the hold up," Lysander says, handing Sage her Visa over the register as he shoots me a wink. She mechanically takes the card, putting it away in her wallet.

"So, how've you been?" I ask, still not sure what to say. Lysander shakes his head, making a hand motion that says I need to say more before walking away.

"Fine, thanks. How about you?" she asks, looking up at me as she switches her bag from her right to left hand.

We stand near the cash register, staring at each other. "Fine. Other than being a front-page celebrity for a day," I murmur. "I had no idea."

"Who I was, or that you'd end up on the front page?" she asks, smiling a little now.

"Both."

"I'm sorry. I guess with the line picking up and the press more interested, nothing's private anymore. I'm truly sorry. I would've warned you if I'd known, but I just, I don't like flaunting that part of who I am, you know? I like to keep it separate."

I nod, understanding and even respecting that. I can imagine she's had issues with men who know who she is only wanting one thing. I'm sort of glad I didn't know who she was because then she knows I wasn't after that one thing. Then again, I'm pretty sure few men look at Sage Everling with her amazing blonde hair and perfect figure and think about money. Not any man with a working cock, that is.

"So, are you following me? Did the press pay you off to get another picture?" she asks pointedly.

"Uh, no. My brother is friends with the owners here. His girlfriend works here."

"So they tipped you off, then?"

Shit, this isn't how I wanted this to go. "No, I just mean I come here a good bit."

"In the what, two weeks, you've lived here, you mean?"

"Well, yes, but they have great pancakes, so I was coming for them."

She nods, wide-eyed, "Oh, I see," she says, clearly mocking me.

"Well, I could ask the same question," I reply. "What are you doing here?"

"Business meeting."

"Oh." Yeah, that didn't really go anywhere.

"But, well, I better get going. I have a meeting with my lead designer and then some phone calls to make. Nice seeing you again, Cash."

"Well, wait a second," I hear myself saying. I just can't imagine letting her walk out that door, can't imagine not seeing her again. I flash back to the other night, the feel of her skin on mine, the expert way she moved, her hair taking on a life of its own as she claimed ownership of my body in a way no woman has before. I think about the connection, about the warm feeling when she was with me. It was more than just sex. It was... I don't know what it was. And I'm sort of scared to know—yet I can't imagine not figuring it out.

"Yeah?" she asks, flipping a strand of blonde hair out of her face.

"What are you doing tonight? I was wondering if maybe you wanted to get dinner."

She smiles. "That's sweet, but that's just not really my thing."

"Eating?" I ask.

"Dating."

I blink. Wow. The player thing's for real. "Why not?"

"I don't have to answer that," she says, shaking her head and preparing to walk away.

"Wait a second," I say, hating how desperate I sound. What the hell's happened to me? Still, as she stands near the door, waiting for my profound statement, I realize it's too late to back down now. "I get it. I do. I'm not one for dating either. With work and with my lifestyle, I'm fine being alone. I'm fine with just sex. In fact, it's sort of my mantra, at the risk of sounding like an asshole."

"I don't think it sounds like you're an asshole. I get it."

"Well, then what's the harm of dinner? Of going out again? The other night was amazing. Why not go for another round?"

She pauses as if she's considering it, her eyes lasering into mine. For a moment, I think I've won her over.

"I had fun, too. Which is exactly why this has to stop there. One night, Cash. That's it. I'm sorry if that makes me seem like a bad person, but it is what it is. I'm focused on my career and work. I like to have fun, but that's it. I'm okay with one-night stands being just that: one night. And as great as you seem and as fun as it was, I just... I can't risk anything more, you know? So thanks, but no thanks. It was good talking to you." And with that, she spins on a heel and opens the door, walking out into the morning air as she leaves me behind in her wake.

"Wow, she's giving you a run for your money. She's going to be a tough one to break," Lysander says, putting a hand on my shoulder.

"Who says I want to break her? Who says I'm going to go after her? I'm fine."

I turn to face Lysander, who is raising an eyebrow. "Sure, you are. That sad puppy face right now is just my imagination. Cash, there's nothing wrong with pursuing something you want, even if it's a little tough. Or Sage Everling tough. I mean, who better to beat her at her own game? You've owned the game for how long now, right?"

He's referring to my player reputation, which we discussed the other night at a bonfire at Wild Hearts. Levi sort of ratted me out to his friends. Not that they're judging. Except for Avery and Jesse, the others have sort of been there before in some version. Just not to my extent.

"Yeah, but I don't know why it matters. I'm not looking for love either."

"Cash, no one goes looking for love. That doesn't mean it can't come to claim you."

"I hardly know her. I mean, I know her body, but not her. She's probably terrible."

"You and I both know you don't believe that. Now get to the booth, and I'll send Georgia out with some pancakes while you think about how you're going to win over Ocean City's truest fashionista."

I want to tell him I'm not going to, that it doesn't matter. I want to tell him that I'm done. But I know it's not true. Because I may have myself convinced I can control my heart, but there's one thing I know without a doubt I can't control—my competitive nature. And it seems like Sage Everling has just challenged me to the biggest competition of my life. I hope she's really ready to play.

ELEVEN

Sage

"I KNOW WHAT YOU'RE DOING," HARPER SAYS. "YOU'RE hoping he's here." Harper leans on Brad at the bar, winking at me in what I find to be an annoying gesture.

"Who?" I ask, raising the margarita to my lips.

"You know who. Cash Creed who."

"That's ridiculous."

"Okay, not to take Harper's side, Sage, but it is rare you'd come here twice in one week, not with things being so busy at work," Brad says now, setting his beer down.

I roll my eyes. "Of course you'll take her side. You two lovebirds. See, see what love does to you? It ruins all original thought. Because of course I'd come here twice in a week with the new line launching. I need to get rid of some stress."

"He's right. Maybe two years ago you'd have been here three or four times in a week, but not now with the business being so serious. But hey, I think it's great. I'm not judging. I think you need to live it up. Your business is a success. You need to take some time to celebrate. But I'm just saying, I know what you're really doing here. You're hoping for a replay."

"That's *so* not true," I reply a little forcefully. "If it were, I'd have accepted his offer for dinner."

"But this way, you can still act under the pretense that you're not interested in him. If you see him here, it'll be a coincidence."

I sigh. I love having a best friend I can tell everything to—like how Cash Creed came into Midsummer Nights and I almost considered saying yes to dinner. But I also hate it because it means I can't hide from myself. Ever. She knows me better than anyone, and she's not willing to let me fool myself.

In truth, though, a big part of the reason I tossed on my favorite silver top and tight jean skirt was in the hopes of seeing Cash Creed. Dammit, I hate what that man's done to me.

It's not just the sex, either. Trust me, I've had plenty of good sex over the years. No, it's something more. Something I can't even explain because... well, what else is there? We had one hot night, and now the man plagues all my daydreams. I keep imagining all these scenarios of running into him, and it's driving me crazy. And then yesterday, the daydream came true and there he was.

When I saw him in front of me, I wanted to take him up on his offer. I imagined what it would be like to get to know him, a man who appreciates both business and play, a man who doesn't take love too seriously but takes pride in his work. He's accomplished, he's driven, and he's a whole hell of a lot of sexy. He knows how to have a good time. He's me in so many ways... but that also scares me.

Because one person hesitant about love is too much in a relationship. Two would be unbearable. So I did the typical Sage Everling tactic—I clammed up, closed myself off, and swore that sex was enough. And then I went home, spent an afternoon when I should've been working daydreaming about how things could've gone differently if I wasn't such a paranoid, antilove kind of woman. What's wrong with me? Don't most women dream about a man like Cash Creed asking her out to dinner?

I know what's wrong with me. It's a mixture of my overly goal-oriented nature mixed with a family background that still haunts me. It's a way to cover my vulnerabilities. My confidence in the bedroom masks what I lack emotionally.

In short, I'm a freaking mess.

But here I am, nonetheless, standing at the bar like a sad excuse for a single lady, keeping my eyes open for one man in particular so I can... what? Awkwardly accept his invitation a day late? Take him to bed for another one-night stand, which will actually be a second-night stand, and then complicate things even more? And who's to say he even feels the same way? He asked me to dinner, not to marry him. The guy clearly is just after more sex, more fun. I don't know why I'm fooling myself.

I think about turning to Harper and Brad and telling them I'm heading home, when Harper smacks my arm, practically knocking the drink out of my hands.

"It's him," she says animatedly, pointing to the door.

I turn to see him walking through. Tonight, he's wearing a suit jacket, charcoal colored. It makes his eyes pop, his hair tousled in a perfectly sexy way. I feel my chest tighten as I set my drink down, trying to remember how to be coy when I really just want to run up to him like a sad sixteen-year-old, squealing and smiling way too much.

But the smiling sixteen-year-old within is quickly squelched. He walks straight through the Marooned Pirate like he's on a mission... and the mission isn't me. I watch him cross the floor to greet a brunette sitting in a corner booth. She stands and extends a hand, which he kisses like he's some Disney prince. She smiles coyly, and he smiles back, squeezing in beside her.

"Oh my God," I say, still staring. I don't know why I'm surprised. I knew this was who he was. And hell, it's who I am too. Why am I so pissed?

"I'm sorry, Sage," Harper says, putting an arm around me. "I'm sorry."

"It's fine," I say, reaching for my drink to toss it back. "It doesn't matter."

"I think it does," she replies. "But look, it's not too late. Why don't you walk on over there, say hi?"

"You know I'm not like that." And I'm not. I'm loose with my own dating rules and sex, but I'm not loose with breaking up relationships, no matter how fresh. Consensual sex between two singles is fine in my books, but any kind of sex when one is attached—just no. That's too complicated.

"Come on, let's get out of here," I say.

"Don't you want to look around? There are some nice guys on the dance floor," she murmurs.

But I'm already gathering my bag and heading toward the door. I've lost my desire to play tonight, and suddenly this life I'm living feels... off. It feels wrong. It feels lousy. So I head out front to snag a cab, anxious to get home to some Netflix and time with the cats.

The life of the rich and famous... oh, how glorious it is.

How gloriously lonely.

TWELVE

Sage
___

I STIR MY SECOND CUP OF COFFEE, ADDING IN WHAT seems like an entire bag of sugar. I need something sweet to get me through this conversation. Seven in the morning is way, way too early to be dealing with this.

"Uh huh," I mumble after counting to ten as Mom continues rambling about the new sheets she ordered and some boat her and Dad were on yesterday and Tahiti and meeting the Queen of England.

Okay, so the last part I may have ad-libbed. But you get the picture.

"Darling, are you even paying attention? I swear, you're so obsessed with that little business venture of yours, you can't even listen anymore."

The little business venture she's referring to is

Evermore. The business I single-handedly built from the ground up without a single ounce of help from my parents—which explains the constant resentment.

"Well, Mom, I *am* busy with Evermore. You know that."

"Your father and I still think it's time to sell that thing before it wears you down. Sell on the up, you know that."

"And you know it's my passion. I'm not selling."

"Oh, darling. You proved your point. You made it. Now quit being so childish."

I roll my eyes. Again, it's too early to deal with my mother. So I suck it up and ignore her, trying to change the subject.

"So when are you two going away?"

"Next week. Want to come?"

"Can't." And it's true. The new line coming up has me busy. But even if I weren't, in truth, I wouldn't be joining Cathy and Alexander Everling anytime soon. That ship has sailed long, long ago. As in at the age of fourteen.

"You know, it saddens me how detached from this family you are, Sage. You're our only daughter, but it's like you don't exist."

"Your words, not mine," I reply, feeling the insolent teenager within rise up.

"You could make some effort, you know."

"Goes both ways, Mom," I reply, shaking my head.

"What did we ever do so wrong, Sage? We gave you everything."

I take a deep breath. She's right. They did give me everything money could buy… and that was about all they gave. But I shove down the childhood problems that come surging back every single time I speak to my mother… which isn't all that often for that very reason. I tell myself it doesn't matter. I made something of myself without them. I stood on my own two feet, and I'm still standing. I am independent, and I'm happy. I don't need their approval, their love, their time. I don't need to be sucked into their world of lavish vacations and showy flashings of money. I'm perfectly content with my life the way it is. Sure, I'm not scraping for money, either, and I can appreciate the finer things in life. But I've worked for it. It wasn't handed to me, not like Dad.

"I'm happy, Mom. Thanks for asking."

"Well, it saddens me that you've walked away from the family. We used to be so close."

The blood starts to boil. I remind myself she's hundreds of miles away, that her words don't matter. But the stubborn, sassy woman within rises up before I can quiet her.

"Really, Mom? And it's my fault that we're not? How about you talk to your husband who has been openly having an affair for fourteen years while you sat by and pretended it didn't matter? Why don't you talk to him about patching back together the façade of the family you two tried to cover with money?"

"Sage...."

But it's too late. There's nothing more to say. I click the phone off, slamming it on the counter. I take a few deep breaths, reminding myself it's irrelevant. I'm not them. I'm different. I'll always be thankful for the upbringing I had. It made me who I am.

A confident businesswoman determined to make a go at it for herself.

A woman who is smart with money but can appreciate it isn't everything.

A woman who isn't going to let the pretense of love own her like it did my mother.

She sat around and watched him flaunt Sheila in front of her for years and did nothing because she knew to walk away from him would be to walk away from the extravagant life they had. She was addicted to money, to the lifestyle he'd built for her—and she let that mean more than her pride.

My parents taught me so many important lessons. They taught me to be independent, to not count on someone to have your back. They taught me that it was okay to be alone because for most of my child-hood, that was what I felt. Most of all, they taught me that love is a weakness, and that love and money are a toxic combination. I won't let that happen to me. I won't let money and love mix. I won't let myself fall into the trap.

Pissed off for the umpteenth time in my life, I grab my purse from the counter and dash out the door, heading to my Sunday ritual, my version of spirituality that helps soothe me, helps remind me I'm nothing like my parents. I get in the car and drive the five miles to my refuge, hoping to work out some of the darkness in my soul and the past.

***

"Hey, sweetheart. How are you?" I murmur, stroking the white cat that's propped over my shoulder.

I'm wearing sweatpants and a ratty old T-shirt from my college days, a far cry from the stylish CEO I try to present to the world. But here, I don't have to be that woman. I don't have to slather on makeup or perfect my outfits. Here is where I let it all go and do something that matters to me.

"Sage, when you're done visiting with Freddy, can you help the family in the waiting room? They're looking for a male cat who is good with kids. Thought you'd have a recommendation," Janice says, peeking around the corner. She's got a mop in her hand.

I smile. "Sure thing. Just a minute."

She grins. "I think you should take Freddy home. Barcelona and Monticello could use a playmate."

I take a deep breath. "You know I would love to. But I'm afraid once I start taking them home from here, I won't be able to stop."

"There are worse things than being a crazy cat lady," Janice replies before spinning around to head back to her cleaning duties.

I suppose she's right.

I gently carry Freddy back to his cage, tucking him in his bed and stroking him once more before heading out to talk to the family. I know exactly the cat that will be their perfect match. Joey, three years old, hit by a car. He's a sweet boy who loves to play and to cuddle. He'll be perfect for a family with kids.

I've got all the stories memorized for the sixty-three cats inhabiting Seaside Serenity Rescue, the animal shelter I volunteer at once a week. I've been coming here every Sunday for five years. It's actually where I adopted Barcelona from when I decided

Monticello needed a friend. Barcelona was born blind, abandoned on the boardwalk. I took one look at him and knew I had to have him. And once I adopted him and saw this place, I knew I had to come back. If I couldn't take every cat home with me, I could at least help place them in homes.

It's my weakness—animals. I've always had a soft spot for them. Coming here, though, is about so much more than serving them. It's about remembering what matters, about escaping from all the pressures of the fast-paced business world. It's about doing something soul soothing.

I stumble out to greet the family, leading them to Joey's cage. An hour later, after they've completed the application and I'm seeing Joey off to his new family, I stand smiling in the office area. I wave to the little girl who is carrying the cat carrier. I know she's got a new best friend. It's beautiful, really.

"Oh, hey Sage, I almost forgot to introduce you to our newest volunteer," Janice calls from the dog room. Janice is the volunteer coordinator and has been working here since the shelter opened in 1982. She's an older woman with a heart of gold. I smile, turning to meet her in the dog room.

"Sage, meet Cash Creed. He just moved here from Texas and loves dogs. He's going to be helping in the dog room on Sundays. Isn't that great?" she says as she motions toward an empty dog pen. Cash is scrubbing it out, getting it ready for the next intake. He stands at the sound of my name, turning to look at me.

"Are you kidding me?" I ask, shaking my head as rage bubbles inside. This is getting ridiculous. I guess it's what I get for one night of fun—I've got myself a stalker.

"Sage? You volunteer here?"

"You know each other?" Janice asks, her sweet smile not calming me. I ignore her, stepping toward Cash.

"Enough is enough. If you don't stop following me, I'll get my lawyer to file a restraining order. And I have a good lawyer, you know." This guy is unbelievable.

Cash shakes his head, laughing. "Full of yourself much? Did you ever think that maybe this has nothing to do with you? That maybe I'm just volunteering?"

"Right. So you just happen to roll into Midsummer Nights the other morning and now you happen to volunteer here on the same day as me?"

"Well, it *is* the only shelter in Ocean City," Janice adds. I turn and give her a look. She puts her hands up in apology, walking with her mop to the other end of the dog room.

"Look, I had no idea you work here. Back home, I

volunteered at our shelter once a week. It's where I adopted Killer, remember him? I thought it might be nice to help out here. I might be an asshole, but I figure volunteering a few hours a week might lessen my asshole score just a tad, you know?"

I roll my eyes. "I still don't know. Mighty coincidental."

"Maybe it's fate," he says, and the smug smirk on his face just irritates me.

"Well, whatever. I'm glad you're helping. You just stay over here in the dog room. I'll stick to the cats."

He leans on the pen now, his arms crossed. He's smirking.

I raise an eyebrow. "What?" I ask. I exhale, still frustrated, but not at the prospect of him stalking me —I'm frustrated at the fact that even in sweats and a T-shirt, scrubbing feces out of a pen, he looks freaking amazing. How can he pull that off? And why is my heart racing so much at the sight of him?

"Just thinking that you look good no matter what you wear... or what you don't."

I open my mouth to protest, but he winks, strolls down the cement walkway, and walks right out the door to the outside area, dogs barking all around us.

I stand in the ruckus, staring at the space where he used to be. Coincidence, stalking, or fate, it doesn't matter. This guy's under my skin. I stomp back to the cat room, needing some time in the cuddle room to get my stress levels down. Sitting back in the cuddle room with Felix this time, stroking his long gray fur, I think about Cash even though I don't want to.

I have to admit, it's nice to know that despite his overt cockiness, he's got some warmth in his heart. I mean, a man who volunteers at a shelter? A man who clearly likes animals? If I were looking for a partner—which I'm clearly not—that would be a big checkmark.

But it doesn't matter. I'm not looking. It's ridiculous to even think about it.

When my shift is done and I'm saying goodbye to my favorites, whispering a silent hope that they find their forever home this week, I hear footsteps coming toward me. I look up to see Cash calmly ambling in the cat room.

I cross my arms. "This is my area."

"I know. But I'm coming to see if you might be willing to switch teams for a half hour."

"What?" I ask, shaking my head.

"I've got three dogs left to walk, and one is quite a handful. Not so good on the leash. I wanted to see if you could give me a hand, take the two little guys so they all get their turn before the shelter closes."

I uncross my arms. "Wait, you walked all the dogs?"

"All fourteen of them."

"How did you manage that in this amount of time?"

"I walked a couple at a time."

"Even Rosco? And Bruiser?" Rosco and Bruiser are our longest residents because, well, let's just say they're not always the friendliest with men.

"Yeah. It was easy. Nothing to it if you're a pro with dogs like me. Now what do you say? Walk with me?"

I roll my eyes, grinning. "How is it that even when you're being charitable, you're arrogant?"

"It's not arrogance if it's founded in reality."

"Whatever."

"So are you in? Or am I going to have to tell Mr. Cheeky and Bobo that they aren't getting a walk today?"

"Fine. One walk. But it's for the dogs."

"Of course," he says, grinning with his hands up. I sigh, following him to the dog room, walking past Janice on the way.

"Glad to see you two getting along," she says, winking.

I shake my head. "We're not."

"If you say so," she says, turning to the filing cabinet as I follow Cash outside to the dog runs.

———

"Maybe you should take him home for Killer," I say as we put Bobo back in his cage, making sure he has food and water an hour later.

"I mean, his name isn't Killer for nothing. Pretty sure Bobo needs a home with a nicer brother."

We've finished our walk, and Janice is getting ready to lock up. I have to admit, even though I'm a self-proclaimed cat lady, spending time out in the sunshine with the three dogs was pretty awesome. Although maybe it was the company I'm keeping.

Walking with Cash was fun and easy. There was no need to impress, no small talk. Just simple fun, laughs, and a whole lot of barking as Cash tried to show off his dog training abilities—and failed miserably.

I say goodbye to Janice as Cash and I walk out to our cars.

"So," he says, hands in the pockets of his sweatpants as he stands near my car.

"So," I repeat.

"Do you maybe want to get a drink? I mean, after

all that barking, I could use something to take the edge off."

"Can't. Sorry."

Cash sighs, rolling his eyes. "Come on. I know it's not your thing. But I'm not half bad, right? I mean, look, you survived an entire hour with me on that walk, and you didn't go running away. That's a good sign, right? I'm not that terrible."

"I never said you were."

"But it's not your thing," Cash murmurs, shaking his head.

"No, drinking is definitely my thing."

"Not with a guy. Too date-like."

"Not in sweatpants when I smell of cat pee and dog kennels."

"Oh," he replies.

"And you're right, too date-like. Wouldn't want you getting the wrong idea. Volunteering together is one thing. Going out for drinks—too risky."

I open my car door, but he puts a hand on it.

"Coffee? How about a cup of coffee? I saw a tiny dump of a shop on the way over here. It's like a block away. Coffee is nonthreatening. Hell, I bet even Janice goes for coffee after work. What do you say? One cup."

I grin. "Do you ever give up?"

"No."

I bite my lip, shaking my head. This seems like a terrible idea. Cash Creed is already worming his way into my life way, way too much. But I don't know. I did like talking to him on the walk. And a cup of coffee seems pretty mild. I have coffee with tons of people in a week.

"One cup. But this isn't a date."

"Obviously," he says. "I mean, look at that outfit you're wearing. I wouldn't be caught dead on a date with a woman dressed like that."

I pinch his arm, but he just laughs. "You're not looking so hot yourself," I reply.

"I think your eyes dancing over me as I was cleaning the kennel say otherwise."

"You're such an ass," I say.

"An ass you're having coffee with."

"Don't push it," I argue. I hop into my car and shut the door, Cash heading to his car. That man is infuriating and ridiculous.

But on the one-block drive to the aptly named Coffee Hole, I find myself grinning stupidly at him, at our day, at our bantering.

It feels good to have a man who can run with me, who can keep up with me. And even if I don't want to admit it, I'm a little excited at the prospect of unwinding for a while, learning more about him, and sipping some probably terrible coffee in a dumpy little shop with a sexy man in sweatpants.

"You better not tell anyone about this. I don't want word getting around that Sage Everling is getting all romantic," I murmur when I get out of my car and follow Cash inside.

"Darling, look at this place. I don't think the word 'romantic' would ever come to mind. If anyone saw us right now, they'd be more likely to think you're involved in a drug ring."

"Lovely thought. You're really winning me over for this coffee thing," I say.

"I don't have to win you over."

"Oh yeah?" I ask as he opens the door to the Coffee Hole, the door screeching at an ear-splitting decibel.

He leans in, whispering. "I think I've already won."

I hit his arm, laughing. "You wish."

I walk over to the counter where a twentysomething is leaning on the dirty counter. There's no one in the place, and it's a good thing—there's exactly one table in the corner. I don't feel clean walking in the place, let alone drinking the coffee. Still, we order two cups and head to the table.

This isn't my kind of place at all, and I don't think it's Cash's either. I smile, though, mentally telling myself it'll all be good. No one's died from a cup of coffee, right?

"This place is atrocious," Cash murmurs.

"This was your idea," I argue.

"Only because you were too busy playing hard to get to agree to go for drinks. Wouldn't margaritas at a decent place be better right now?"

My mouth waters a little at the thought of margaritas. "Pretty sure we're dressed for Coffee Hole, not margaritas at a nice bar.

"We could always change, meet up later," he says.

"Nice try," I reply.

"Was it? Because that wasn't even my best."

I roll my eyes as the barista—if we can call a dazed dude in a T-shirt who poured some coffee into a Styrofoam cup a barista—brings our coffee over. It looks like tar in a cup.

"Maybe we should just call it a night," I note, looking into my cup with disgust.

"Don't be ridiculous. I just bought you an amazing cup of coffee. The least you could do is chat with me while we both pretend we're going to take a sip of this stuff. Come on, it's not so bad. Tell me about you, won't you? I mean, I at least deserve to know something about the woman who was grinding all over me on the front-page of the paper."

I smile, studying him. His dark eyes peer back at me, and I feel my heart beat a little faster. "Well, what do you want to know?"

He studies me for a long moment before speaking. "Everything."

"Is that all?" I ask, teasing.

"I'll settle for anything right now," he says.

I shrug, thinking. "Well, let's see. I'm obsessed with Ed Sheeran. He's probably the only man I'd consider marrying, even though he's already engaged so that's off the table. I have two cats, a hairless cat named Monticello after my favorite vacation spot and a blind cat named Barcelona whom I adopted from Seaside Serenity. I love pancakes, coffee, and orange soda. They're my guilty pleasures. And I also like making pottery, although I haven't really had time lately with the business picking up. My parents are both assholes whom I don't really talk about because it just pisses me off. I'm an only child, my business is everything to me, and that's about it."

He smiles at me.

"What?" I ask, realizing I've probably overshared. I think this is more than I've ever told man about me in like five years.

"Nothing. It's just nice to finally meet you. Kind of

backwards, you know? I get carnal knowledge of you before I know your favorite food."

"Well, don't get any ideas. This doesn't mean anything. I'm not—"

He covers my hand with his, and I jolt at the electricity of his skin on mine. "I know. Me neither. Will you relax a little? Jesus, it's not an audition for marriage. Just wanted to get to know you a little, since we'll be volunteering together and all."

I take a breath, easing back into my seat, staring at him.

"Your turn," I say.

He proceeds to tell me about his apartment back in Texas, his family, and his favorite television shows. It's simple, really, the two of us in a dive of a coffee shop, not drinking a single sip of coffee, talking about little things that mean a lot.

When an hour has passed and the seemingly stoned barista tells us it's closing time—at six o'clock —Cash walks me to my car.

"I had fun today," he says.

I shield my eyes from the sun. "Me too," I admit.

"Friends?" he asks, extending a hand. "Or is that against the rules, too?"

"I don't know. I don't have a rule for that. I usually don't see my lays more than once," I admit, smiling.

"Sage Everling, you've got a heart of steel. Has anyone ever broken through it?" he asks me.

I stare at him defiantly. "Never," I confess.

"Well, I'm not one to give up, you know?"

I open my mouth in protest, but before I can say anything, he's pinning me up against the door of my car, his mouth pressed against mine. I want to stop him, my head telling me this isn't a good idea. But as his hand moves through my hair in just the perfect way, as he takes ownership of me with his lips, I ease into it.

He's a little bit aggressive and a whole lot of confident.

He's the alpha to my alpha, and it's just the way I like it.

It's a power struggle with this one, both of us trying to take the reins.

Somehow, though, the tug-of-war works. I like it, I admit to myself.

I like him.

Just when I find my hands wandering to his hips, thinking about how good it would feel to let him take me in the backseat, he pulls away.

"See you later," he says, calmly strolling away, leaving me breathless against my car, wondering what the hell just happened. He shoots me a smile and a wink before climbing into his car and driving away.

I open the car door and slump into the seat, resting my head on the steering wheel.

Damn, that man's good.

For a moment, I almost thought maybe I was going to break my rules. I shake my head, wondering what game Cash Creed is up to and how I'm going to beat him at it.

THIRTEEN

Cash

AFTER TAKING CARE OF SOME PAPERWORK AT THE condos and the apartments, I head over to Wild Hearts on Monday evening to see Levi. When I get there, I take a seat at Midwestern Nights, the café attached to the horse-riding coral, and listen to Reed animatedly chatting with customers.

"Hey," he says once he's finished selling a couple some Texas sheet cake from the display. On a typical day, he runs Midwestern Nights here with Levi. It's a branch of his husband Lysander's Midsummer Nights. "What are you up to?"

"Just stopped by to see Levi. Wanted to check the place out."

"He's on the trail with a group of fourteen-year-olds here for a birthday party."

I shake my head. "Sounds like hell."

"That's what I thought too. Especially after our day. We had a group come over from the senior center this morning. That was a trip."

"Glad to hear things are busy. It's good to see Levi's dreams coming true again."

I mean it. It was a rough year the year he had his accident. Although I never quite understood the bronc riding thing, I did understand his devastation when it ended. It's good to see my big brother picked himself up, dusted himself off Creed style, and rebuilt his life with a new dream.

"You want some sheet cake while we wait for him to get back?" he asks.

"Probably should watch my figure. Haven't been to the gym since I got here."

"Please. That figure's looking fine to me. I'm sure Miss Everling would agree."

I roll my eyes. "I swear. Can we have just one conversation that doesn't involve her?"

"Get me one of those new bags I'm hearing about before they hit the store online, and maybe."

"I don't think that's in the cards for you."

"A man can dream."

"That he can," I say as Reed winks, rushing to the display case to pull me out some Texas sheet cake. He brings it over and slides it to me on the table, sitting across from me.

"Damn, that's good," I say after a couple of bites. "Maybe even better than Mama's. Just don't tell her."

"Thanks," he says, beaming as I wolf down the rest of the dessert.

"So," I say through a mouthful of cake. "What's new with you and Lysander?"

Reed shrugs. "Can you keep a secret?"

"No. Not really."

He raises an eyebrow. I shrug. "Just being real. But go ahead. I'll give it my best."

"We're going through training to become foster parents."

"What? Are you serious? That's wonderful, man," I say, putting down my fork.

"Yeah. I mean, there was a time I wasn't sure about being a dad, but being with Lysander, it's really shown me that it's possible, that I *can* be a dad. And I thought who better to understand what it's like being a foster child than me? Since I grew up in it, I know exactly what it feels like. I think that could really help me help out other kids going through it."

"That's beautiful. I know I don't know you that well, but it's going to be great. Listen, I know things can get tricky. If you ever find yourself needing legal advice, you know, to look over paperwork or whatever, you know where to find me."

"Thanks," he smiles. "We haven't told anyone else yet. We just want to wait until we get through training and all, until it's official."

"I won't say a word," I reply. It's kind of cool that Reed trusted me with this even though I'm not really on the inside of the group yet. Of course, maybe that's why he trusted me. No risk when you don't know someone that well.

"Won't say a word about what?" a voice bellows from the door. We turn.

"What happened to the party?" Reed asks, standing.

Levi shakes his head. "The girls thought it was too hot out, and the mom who was with them wouldn't stop whining. Said she wasn't an outdoorsy kind of person. I mean, judging by the stilettos she wore to go horse riding, I sort of got that. Anyway, they decided to cut it short."

"Sorry," Reed says, grimacing.

"I'm not. God, it's been one hell of a day."

"Want a beer?" Reed asks.

"Bring us a round," Levi nods, taking a seat across from me now. "And what is Ocean City's finest landlord doing here? You come to ride a horse, brother?"

"You wish. No, just thought I'd stop and see how things were going."

"Busy. Busier than hell. I'm glad I have you here to run the other end of things."

"Don't get used to it. You know...."

"You're just here for summer. I know. Unless that Sage character bangs you enough to make you want to stay longer."

"Or marries him," Reed yells.

"Listen, you know me, brother. You know that's not my game."

"Sometimes the game changes," he says, readjusting the hat on his head.

"Not this time," I say, shaking my head, shoving aside the afternoon I spent with Sage yesterday, the slight breaking of my own rules.

"So did you see her again?" Levi asks.

I sigh. "Why so much interest in my love life? Last I heard, you have your own."

"Truth. But Mama's paying me good money to keep tabs on you," Levi says. I'm not completely sure he's teasing.

"Well, if you must know, yeah, I saw her. At the animal shelter yesterday."

"You're volunteering there?" Reed asks, joining us in the booth.

"Yeah, what can I say?"

"Sexy, confident, and an animal lover? No wonder the women swoon for you. Levi, maybe you're lucky you got here first. Maybe Jodie would have went for this one."

Levi punches Reed in the arm as I laugh.

"So did you sleep with her again?" Levi asks.

"No. I'm playing things a little differently."

"Oh yeah?"

"Yeah."

"As in...." Levi says, waiting for me to fill in the blank.

"It's not a big deal. I just took her for coffee. Talked a little. I think women like Sage need a different approach. I wooed her a bit, teased her a bit, and then pulled the old hard to get card. We'll see if it works."

"You know, some would be bothered by your irreverent discussion of games and love."

"This is me you're talking to. You weren't always a stranger to the game."

"What game? Are we playing Cards Against Humanity Again?" another voice asks. We turn to see Jodie strolling through.

"Oh, that one's fun. Remember that card your mom played?" Reed asked.

Jodie groans. "Don't remind me. How's it going, Cash?"

"What, Cash gets a hello before me?" Levi asks, shaking his head.

"You get all kinds of hellos, did you forget?" Jodie asks.

"That's my cue to get home to my hubby," Reed says, hands in the air.

"Oh please. There's not a single person here who is a prude. Not a single one." Jodie says, shaking her head.

"Interesting. We were just talking about Cash's sexual prowess," Reed says as he heads to the back to clean up.

"It was more like an interrogation," I murmur.

"Oh, is it that Sage chick? Damn, she's smoking. You see her again?" Jodie asks, taking Reed's seat.

"Yeah. At the shelter. Went for coffee."

"Coffee? That's the best you could do?" she asks, smiling.

"Listen, that woman's a handful. It was like pulling teeth to get her to agree to a single cup."

"Oh, she's good. The old hard-to-get act. Nice," Jodie announces, smirking.

"Sounds like you're speaking from experience,"

Levi says, putting an arm around her as she leans into him.

"Well, we all have our ways," she says, shrugging.

"So, when are you going to see her again?" Levi asks.

"Next week probably. At the shelter."

"And in the meantime?"

"In the meantime, I might give that Layla a call."

"You two-timer," Jodie says, feigning horror.

"It's not two-timing when you're not a thing. Nothing's changed. Sage is fun and smart and gorgeous. And yeah, I had fun talking to her. But it doesn't change anything. I've still got my Cash Creed game, and I'm ready to play."

Levi rolls his eyes. "You're hopeless. Just admit this one's got a hold of you somehow."

"Well, that's impossible," I say, standing from the table. "No one can catch this guy. Now, I'm off to the bachelor pad. I'm tired. I'll see you tomorrow. I want to talk about that new rental agreement you showed me. Some of the wording leaves loopholes."

"Well, maybe, instead of looking for loopholes in the rental agreement, you should be searching for loopholes in your own love life rules. Maybe a girl like Sage Everling is what you need, you know?" Jodie asks, raising an eyebrow.

"Even if that were true, which it's not, that woman isn't going to bend. If you think I'm tough with my rules, you should see hers."

"Show up on her doorstep. Surprise her. I'm sure you can work that Texan charm."

"One problem. I have no clue where she lives. And although I'm all about living a little dangerously, not sure I want a stalking lawsuit slapped on me."

"You're a lawyer. You could get out of it."

I shake my head, waving goodbye as I head out the door, thinking about what Jodie said.

Thinking about Sage.

Thinking about how many days until I see her again and wondering how the hell I'm going to find a loophole in my own heart to get me out of this train wreck before it crashes into me.

***

"So, not to bring up your love life again, but how bad do you want that Sage Everling back in your bed?" the voice asks when I answer my phone the next afternoon.

"Reed?"

"Yeah, it's me. And I've got some hot news for you. I was scrolling through Instagram this morning, stalking my favorite designers, and one Sage Everling's latest post showed up. Apparently, she has this hairless cat named Monticello who escaped last night from her condo. She's offering a huge reward for information leading to the return of her cat."

I sigh, thinking about how she was in the cat room at the shelter. I have a feeling that cat means everything to her, judging by her baby talk with the cats and the fact she volunteers there.

"Well, lucky for me, I have a job, so I don't really need a reward," I say.

"Listen. Imagine how grateful she'll be if you find that cat. I mean, the cash reward would probably accompany a huge thank you, gratitude, who knows what else for the right guy. This would totally win her over. Plus, who knows, maybe she'd like throw in a bag or something."

I shake my head looking at the ceiling. "So are you sure you don't want to find the cat?"

"Well, trust me, I've been searching the area around Midsummer all morning. But I thought if we team up, we have a chance to find the damn naked cat. You could get more time with her to do whatever it is you crazy kids want to do, all Christian Grey style or whatever, and I could get my bag."

"I'd hardly call our sex Christian Grey level. Yet," I add, grinning to myself.

"Hey, no one's judging. But the point is this. Get over here and help me find this cat, and maybe we both could get what we want."

I sigh, leaning on my counter. "Even if I was so desperate to win Sage over, finding a cat in Ocean City isn't exactly the easiest task. It's like a needle in a haystack and all that."

"Well, exactly. But with our two brilliant minds, maybe we have a shot. I messaged Sage on Insta to ask what streets she lost him between. It's 78th and Baltimore."

"Shit, that's right near my condo."

"Bingo. So we have a starting point."

So Sage Everling lives within a block of me. Interesting. She completely failed to mention that one. Hell, we could carpool together.

"Are you listening?" Reed asks, bringing me back to the conversation. "I said I'll meet you at your condo in fifteen if that's okay. I'll bring some tuna. Get your kitty-calling voice ready. We're finding this cat if it kills us."

He hangs up before I can protest. Great. Not exactly how I wanted to spend my day—sweating in the hot summer sun creeping around with Reed looking for a naked cat that's probably either squashed or long gone. What the hell has life come to? People accuse Texas of being weird, but this place isn't really selling itself as normal these days.

I sit back on the couch, thinking about all the things I could be doing this afternoon—work, getting an early start at the bar, or more likely, lying on the beach staring at scantily clad women all day. Instead, I'm waiting for another man to come over so we can go whistle for a cat all day. Just great. This woman isn't my girlfriend. Hell, she was a one-night stand, and look at all the trouble she's causing. I've got to get with it, put my foot down, and move on. This isn't the kind of thing I do.

Twenty minutes later, Reed shows up at the door. "Hey, Cash, good news. I've been thinking this whole way here. I know exactly where to start," Reed announces as he barrels through my door without even knocking.

I shake my head. "This ought to be good."

"Michael's Crab Shack," he blurts. "Come on, it makes sense. It's right near where Sage lives, and you can smell that place from here. If I were a cat, I'd be dumpster diving there."

I raise an eyebrow. "And you think Sage hasn't thought of this?"

"Have you seen Michael's Crab Shack? The place looks like you'd get crabs walking by it. Doesn't seem like the kind of place a woman like her would think of."

I shake my head. "So what, we're going to just go scope the place out for a cat?"

"You got it. Now come on. Time's wasting."

I pinch the top of my nose between my thumb and forefinger. "Okay, let's go," I say because I really don't know what else to say. I follow Reed out into the summer air, passing a poster of the missing cat in question. As we walk the several blocks to our dilapidated location, I think about how in Texas, I'd never be going dumpster diving for a cat. I guess a whole lot can change in the blink of an eye

"Here, Monticello. Here kitty," Reed yells, crouched behind the dumpster as I gag, trying not to hurl from the smell of rotten seafood. I'm not sure if the smell is actually coming from the dumpster or from inside this place.

I cover my nose with my sleeve. "If Monticello knows what's good for him, he'll pick a bit of a classier place to dumpster dive. Shit, this place stinks." I cough, Reed still searching around the dumpsters for the cat he's convinced is here. Looks like Monticello has finer tastes than this.

"What are you two doing back here? Do I need to call the police?" a voice bellows from behind me. I turn to see a man in an apron splattered with all sorts of food standing in a doorway. I put my hands in the air in a sign of innocence, as if he's the police. This only makes me feel more idiotic.

"Just looking for a missing cat," Reed says smoothly, coming over to stand beside me.

The guy, sporting a moustache that is enviable if not a bit over-the-top, rolls his eyes. "Yeah, you and everyone else on the block. Never seen a damn search party so big for a freaking cat. There have been seven people back here today looking for some cat, hoping for some reward or something. Honestly, what, is the cat the Pope's or something?"

"Better. Sage Everling," Reed replies.

"Who?"

"Never mind," I say. "Sorry for trespassing. We'll be going now."

The man wipes his hands on his apron and returns inside, muttering something about no-good tourists.

"Well, I think he needs to work on his charm a bit if he wants Michael's to take off," Reed says, wiping his hands as if he's ridding himself of Michael's Crab Shack

"So now what, master cat finder?"

Reed sighs. "I really thought this was our lucky break."

"Well, you heard Michael or whoever that guy was. There's already a search party in full force. I'm sure someone is going to beat us to finding the cat."

"Someone's a bit cynical."

"Realistic. Now, how about we head to Midsummer Nights, get ourselves a drink, and let someone else do the work."

Reed is glum as we walk toward Midsummer Nights. "There goes my lovely bag or sneak peek at the men's line."

I shake my head. "All this for a bag? Wow."

He jabs me in the ribs, grinning. "All this for a woman? Wow."

"I was just helping you. This wasn't about her."

"Keep telling yourself that, darling," he says, grinning as we walk toward the restaurant, hands in our pockets, the summer sun blazing.

"Where have you two been?" Levi asks, sitting at the bar when we return.

"What are you doing here? Don't you have a business to run?" I ask.

"Same goes for you," Levi replies as Lysander slides him a beer. "I shut down for the day. Wanted to give the staff a break. Jodie's working on her latest book at home, so I thought I'd come to my second favorite place."

Reed and I both grab a stool at the bar, and Lysander slides us each a drink as well.

"If we'd have known, you could've come with us. I bet with all your rodeo skills, you'd be perfect at wrangling him." Reed takes a swig of the beer, winking at Lysander.

"Wrangling who?" Levi asks.

"Monticello," Reed replies. "We needed a wrangling expert or a freaking miracle to find it."

"Why do you two smell a little weird? No offense," Lysander says now, shriveling his nose up.

"You two do smell a little ripe," Levi replies.

"We were dumpster diving at the crab shack," I say.

"Little brother, you have some new hobbies you need to enlighten me about? Dumpster diving doesn't quite seem like your scene."

"Well, it is if it gives him the chance to win Sage Everling over," Reed adds, and I shoot him a look.

"Oh, did you two find Monticello?" Lysander asks.

"No. I told Reed it was useless," I say. "There are already a ton of people looking for him. But Reed was convinced he'd be in the dumpster at the crab shack."

"Makes sense, right?" Reed asks, jumping to his own defense.

"I think it was worth a shot," Lysander replies, leaning across the bar to kiss him. "I love you, even if you do smell a little odd. How about you head home and grab a shower? Maybe I could take a break, get Joseph to run the bar."

"Oh, I could use some company," Reed murmurs.

"Do you two ever simmer down?" Levi asks.

"What fun would that be? Now, you two boys, behave. And Cash, keep your eyes open. You never know when opportunity could just drop into your lap. A cat can only be in so many places, you know?" Reed says, slapping my back as he leaves.

I shake my head, drinking my beer as the two rush out like teenagers. It's just me and Levi at the bar now.

Levi smirks. "So, dumpster diving for cats now? Man, brother, she's got you good, real good."

"What are you talking about? This was Reed's idea. I was just helping him out."

"Uh huh. You tell yourself that. You tell yourself you weren't trying to be the hero, save the day so Sage gives you another chance. Oh, shit. You're done for. I'll get my wedding toast ready."

I elbow him. "Keep dreaming. I was just being nice. There are plenty of fish in the sea I haven't tested out yet."

"Yeah, but there's only one who has you hooked."

"No one beats this fisherman at his game."

"We'll see about that," Levi says before heading around the bar to get himself another beer.

***

THE REST OF THE WEEK PASSES BY AT A STEADY PACE. I call in the plumber for some repairs at the condo and show a few apartments off to some newcomers. I go to the club a few times, but no one really piques my interest. I also spend a morning on the sand, taking in the scenery—the ocean waves and the women. Okay, maybe the bikinis get my attention a little more if I'm being honest. And, if I'm being honest, I do spend a little more time than usual scoping out my surroundings for a certain cat with creepily wrinkled tan skin. I find myself peeking behind bushes and turning my head when I heard a meow.

But no luck. No Monticello. No chance at another night with Sage.

When Sunday rolls around, my day at the shelter, I have to admit there's a little bounce in my step. Maybe Sage will need a shoulder to cry on. Maybe she'll need a bed to wash away her sadness over her lost cat. Or, at the very least, maybe she'll need a cup of coffee from a dilapidated building where no one will recognize her. Of the three choices, I know which one I'm hoping for —but I'll take any of the above.

In truth, I spent a little more time getting ready, slicking the hair back just right. I traded in my typical shelter outfit of sweatpants and a T-shirt for some nicer fitting jeans. I put on some extra cologne.

I get to the shelter and Janice gives me instructions, showing me to the new intake area where I can help get a few new pups settled in.

"Sage here yet?" I ask, trying to be nonchalant.

"She's not coming in today," Janice says, smiling.

I try to keep a poker face. Apparently I fail.

"She's a special one, that Sage, isn't she? It's rare to find a woman who is pretty, super successful, but super sweet, too. None of that fame and fortune went to her head, you know? I do hope she can find someone who appreciates that," she says, winking at me.

"Yeah, she seems okay," I say as I lean down to let Chopper, a tiny Yorkie, out of his kennel and take him for a walk.

"For a man who thinks she's just okay, you seem pretty despondent. But none of my business, really. Carry on." With that, she whisks herself off to the cat room, leaving me standing with the tiny dog, grimacing. She's right. I *am* embarrassingly despondent. And I hate that I'm despondent. What the hell is wrong with me?

At that, Chopper decides he can't wait to get outside to the grass, peeing all down the front of me. Peeing all over my expensive jeans I wore to impress a woman who isn't even here.

"Great," I mutter, exhaling as the dog licks my face, his butt wiggling in happiness.

At least someone is having a good day.

I'M FINISHING UP SOME FILING IN THE OFFICE WHEN I hear the door fly open. An old man hobbles in, leaning heavily on a cane. He's wearing a fedora and thick glasses. A cigar hangs from his mouth.

"We're closing soon, sir," I say, looking up from the folder in my hand.

"Got something for you," he murmurs, his voice gruff.

Shit. An intake right before closing. Not the kind of depressing note I want to leave on. I hate seeing animals come in.

"We have a form for a surrender you'll have to fill out," I say, rifling through the other folder where the forms are.

"I'm not surrendering anything. It's something I found. A stray, I guess. Weird, though. The thing must be sick or something."

"What is it?" I ask.

"Cat. Sick cat. No hair."

At this, I freeze. "Did you say no hair?"

"You need a hearing aid, boy? I said no hair. Now are you going to come get the mangey thing or what? Found it scavenging in my garbage can behind my house. Thought it was a coon at first. I always hated cats, to tell you the truth. But decided to do a good deed and drive it down here. At my age, you need all the heaven points you can get. Now come get it before it pukes in my car or something."

I can hardly believe it as I follow him to his station wagon. I peer in the backseat window, where a box sits. Inside, a tan hairless cat with a blue collar lets out a meow.

Monticello.

"Monticello! Hey, thanks, buddy. Thanks a ton," I say, reaching out a hand toward the guy. He groans, climbs into his car, and tosses the cane on the passenger seat.

"Good luck," he says as I open the back door to grab the box, careful not to stir Monticello too much. The old guy is backing out before I'm even back in the gate to the shelter.

"Hey, buddy. Where have you been? Oh, this is good luck." I wander inside as Janice emerges from the cat room.

"What do you have there?" she asks as I approach the counter, putting the box down.

She looks inside. "Oh my, is that…?"

"Monticello. Sage's Monticello," I say, beaming.

She smiles. "Oh, thank God. She's going to be so relieved.

"Can you call her?" I ask, knowing she needs to know right away. I know I'd want to know immediately if this were Killer.

"No," she says, smiling. "You can just take him to her."

"Me? I don't think that's a good idea," I say, tossing the idea around in my head. Won't it be weird for me to show up? I don't want her thinking I'm super creepy or odd.

Although, showing up with her beloved cat at her condo might not be such a bad idea. The gratitude, the appreciation—there's no way she's choosing a cup of coffee to celebrate.

"It's a perfect idea. Here, I'll give you her exact address. Now get going, there's no time to waste. This cat means so much to her, and I think she'll be super excited to see him. And you."

"Janice...." I shoot her a pointed look.

"Oh, please, Cash. Drop the macho act. From the second I saw you two in here together, I knew you were crazy about her. And I knew she was crazy about you. Will you two stop being fools and just get on with it?"

I smile, shaking my head as she finds a carrier to put Monticello in. I don't have the heart to tell Janice we've already got on with it in one way, been there done that. I just don't really want to have that conversation with her. Still, as I drive Monticello to my condo so I can clean up first—I don't think dog piss will naturally lend itself to a bedroom kind of thank-you, if you know what I mean—I think about what she said. I think about how maybe Sage Everling isn't the total player she pretends to be. I think that maybe, like me, she can be beaten at her own game.

<hr />

MY HEART POUNDS AS I STAND AT THE DOOR TO 704, the cat carrier in my right hand as I knock with my left hand.

"Coming," a smooth voice says, and I take a deep breath. I wonder what she's wearing. I wonder how she'll react. I wonder so many things.

The door opens, and there she is, hair in a simple bun. She's wearing tight jeans and a red top, her blue eyes sparkling.

"Cash?" she inquires, taking a step back. But then her gaze lands on the carrier in my hand and she gasps.

"Monticello?" she asks now, leaning down to peer in the carrier. Her beloved cat lets out a guttural cry, and she quickly ushers me in, tears falling. I step inside her abode. Perhaps the better word is oasis.

Everything is airy and clean, bright white floors and walls accented by earthy-toned decorations. There's an eclectic yet elegant vibe happening, from the black marble countertops to the chandelier in the living room. It's sophisticated and beautiful, but not over-the-top. It's a balance between expensive taste and simplicity, and it works.

Sage is opening the door to the carrier, tears falling freely now as she scoops up her beloved cat.

"I can't believe it. Baby, where have you been?"

As the reunion continues, another cat ambles out from the living room meowing. It walks toward me, and I think it's going to rub my leg. Instead, it runs headfirst into me, stumbles, and shakes its head.

"Sorry. That's Barcelona. He's blind."

"Oh, whoops. Sorry," I say awkwardly to the cat, wondering what the hell I'm supposed to do. Why do I feel so out of my element?

I reach down to pet the cat, who purrs. Sage puts down Monticello, and the two cats have a reunion complete with rubbing, hissing, and then eventually running off to another part of the condo.

"Where'd you find him?" she asks, wiping away the tears. I think about what Reed would want me to say, about how he'd want me to lie. I opt for the truth. Again, I'm an asshole, but not a total one.

"The shelter. An elderly man brought him in. Found him in his trash out back. Janice asked me to bring him to you."

"Well, thank you. Thank you so much," she says, shaking her head. "I've been worried sick. I know he's just a cat, but he's so much more to me. I've had him for five years now."

I grin as she leads me into the living room, asking if I want a drink.

"I'm fine."

We sit on her sofa, awkwardly. Finally, I break the silence. "So, why hairless?"

It's the only question that comes to mind. Definitely not a question in my repertoire.

She smiles. "Because I always wanted one. Since I was little. My parents wouldn't get me a cat. My mother said she didn't want cat hair everywhere. So, I asked for a hairless cat. Mom said they were the ugliest creatures she ever saw. When I got in the position to be able to afford one, it was the first thing I bought." She smiles big.

"I take it pissing off your mother is at the top of your hobby list?" I ask.

"You got it," she says, winking and then laughing. "I'm a pro at it too. Although it isn't hard. There are millions of ways to accomplish it, mostly doing something that insinuates you're poor. Like buying items that aren't name brand or wearing sweatpants in public. Mom's all about the image."

"Interesting," I say, not sure what else to say.

Sounds like there's a lot going on with the family. A lot of baggage.

"Not really. I try not to interact with my family that much anymore. But that's a long story. You didn't come here to hear about my mom dramas. Thank you again."

"No problem. Really. I'm glad he's home."

We sit again, close enough on the couch that I could reach out and touch her. I think about it, wonder if she's thinking about it too. Just sitting here, I can feel the tension between us, the chemistry radiating. I think about that night, how our bodies moved so perfectly, how her confidence just got me going. I think about what it would be like to take her on this perfectly white couch, right in the airy living room.

I run a hand through my hair, exhaling. "I should probably get going," I say, shaking my head. This is dangerous territory.

Levi's right. This woman has me hooked—and I've got to rip out the hook before it sinks in deeper.

She nods. "Yeah, I've got some work to do. Oh, who am I kidding. I'm going to go sit with Monticello for hours watching Netflix and being thankful he's back."

I smile. "Sounds like fun."

I walk to the door, hands in my pockets. I turn as she

stares. She's biting her lip, her gaze studying me. She opens her mouth as if she's going to ask something but then apparently changes her mind. I wonder if she was going to ask me to stay. I wonder if I would've said yes.

"Thanks again, Cash. It was good seeing you."

"You too. See you at the shelter?"

"See you next Sunday, yep. Oh, and I almost forgot. Your reward."

I perk up, wondering if she's changed her mind, wondering if my cologne is working its magic.

"Just let me get my purse," she says as she turns.

I sigh. Money. She means the money.

"Hey, no way. Don't worry about it. Besides, I didn't find him anyway."

"Are you sure?"

"Positive."

"I'll just donate the reward to the shelter," she says.

I nod, thinking about how Reed would kill me right now for not asking for a bag.

As I open the door and step out of her condo, though, I'm really not thinking about rewards or bags. I'm thinking about how much I want her to ask me to stay—and how much that scares me. I turn and see her standing in the doorway. From where I'm standing, I can smell her floral perfume. It smells amazing, sensuous. Now I'm biting my lip.

"Bye," she says, and even that one word rustles through me. She smiles and clicks the door shut. For a moment I stand, staring at the door, exhaling. I spin on my heel and head off, grabbing my cell phone from my pocket.

I dial Levi. "Hey, you and Jodie busy tonight? Wondering if you want to go out."

"It's Sunday night."

"And? Are you a grandpa or something? Having pot roast with the kids? Come on. What better way to start the week?"

"Not all of us are party animals lately. Don't you ever just want a quiet night at home?"

I think about it. "Not tonight I don't. Come on."

"Is that Cash?" I hear a bubbly voice yell from the background. "Does he want to go out?"

"See, even Jodie knows I'm good for a good time."

Levi sighs. "All right. But just one drink."

"That's what they all say," I murmur as I click the phone, feeling better about getting out, getting back to my comfort zone.

FOURTEEN

Sage

"So what was his reward?" Harper asks, winking at me. We're out for coffee Monday morning. We're supposed to be reviewing some marketing plans and some design elements, but as usual, our meeting has turned into a love life gossip session. And the focus is, as usual, me.

"Nothing. I just said thank you."

"With your body?" Harper asks, giggling.

"Harper, really. Are you fifteen?"

"Sage, really, are you a hundred? Come on. You know the man only drove the whole way over because he thought returning your cat would score him some points."

"And it did. I was very appreciative."

"So you didn't think about jumping his bones? Not once?" she asks.

I roll my eyes, taking a sip of coffee. Harper is easily distracted. Maybe she'll change the subject. After a long swallow of coffee, though, she's still sitting across from me, blinking. I sigh.

"Okay, yes, he smelled amazing. And his outfit looked good. I'd sort of forgotten how good he looks. But it was just physical, nothing more."

"So why didn't you invite him to stay, to get physical?"

"Because. I don't want him getting any ideas."

"What? Like that you like him?"

"I don't like him."

She raises an eyebrow at me. I can't lie. Even I can hear how weak my assurance is.

"Look, he seems like an okay guy. But you know I don't have time for this. What, are we going to spend the summer going out to dinner and to the movies? He'll buy me flowers, and I'll confess my love to him... and then what? We'll spend maybe six months or a year together; we'll get bored or fight over money or realize we're not compatible, and it'll be over? I'll be crying into a tub of ice cream, buy another cat to cover my sadness, and think about all the wasted time and effort? What's the point? Why not just skip over it all, enjoy the fun parts, and forget about the rest?"

"I swear, Sage Everling, you should've been a man. You are the most emotionless woman I know."

"Thanks."

"I mean it. Don't you ever want to just let your heart go? To experience passion and loyalty and connection? Don't you ever feel like that's missing?"

I consider her words for a minute. "Yeah. But then I remember the other assholes I gave a chance. I think about how many months I cried over Kevin and how many times I got pissed over Mark. I think about all the suffering, all the distraction, and I realize this whole sex and nothing more thing is perfect."

"Well, I don't care what you say. Cash Creed isn't like Kevin or Mark. For one, he's way hotter. And two, I think he could keep you interested much longer than a year. Plus, I think no matter what you tell yourself, you're interested. You like him. So stop being all crazy."

I stir my coffee, wondering why my chest feels heavy. I hate this. I hate that Harper's sort of right. I hate that all night last night, I was in bed thinking about how things could be different if I'd have asked the question I wanted to ask, if I'd have asked Cash to stay. I think about what it would've been like to wake up in his arms this morning, to make breakfast for him and to drink coffee on the balcony. I think about how good it would feel to share my fears and worries, my dreams for Evermore with someone besides just my employees.

I brush it off. It's stupid. It's senseless. Even if I could get over this whole fear, who says *he* could?

"It doesn't matter, anyway," I say. "Because I'm going out tonight."

"With who?"

"That PR manager from our fabric distributor, Steven. He's going to the club tonight, some party. Asked if I want to stop by."

"Wait, is this that hippie-trippy guy with the long black ponytail?"

"That's him."

"He's so not your type."

"Who says hippie isn't my type? He's into business. He's sexy."

"You know this is just a rebound."

"How can you rebound when you serially aren't dating?" I ask, rolling my eyes.

"You know what I mean. This is so you can convince yourself Cash Creed means nothing."

"He doesn't."

"Thank God you're a much better business owner

than liar. Because that was the suckiest lie I've ever heard. But whatever. I hope Steven gives you a rocking good time tonight."

"I'm sure he will. Now, about those designs...." I say, shoving my coffee to the side so she can unfold her portfolio.

"About the designs that are going to skyrocket us to the top," Harper says, animatedly. I love seeing her passion for her work.

I think about that, about how Harper lives her life with passion. Her relationship with Brad, her work—she puts everything on the table quite literally. It must be freeing to live like that. Then again, she's had quite a different upbringing and quite a different view of love.

Two parents who are madly in love thirty-seven years after tying the knot. A simple upbringing with dinners at the table, cousins over for the holidays, and playing in the backyard. She learned early on that love didn't hurt, and that life was about finding companionship.

As she talks about hemlines and stitches, I try to listen, try to block out the self-pitying notions about how life could be so much different if I'd have had parents different from mine. Then again, is it fair to blame them for everything? Is it truly their fault I'm an ice queen when it comes to matters of the heart? Is it completely their fault that my perfectionist tendencies mixed with my pessimism about love make me so afraid to get hurt?

I don't know. There's a whole hell of a lot I don't know.

But I do know Steven will be a good distraction tonight, and God knows I need that right about now.

FIFTEEN

Sage

"So, dance, drinks, or both?" Steven asks me as I stroll into the Marooned Pirate on his arm. I've got my sky-high stilettos on and some jeans so tight I can barely breathe. His jet-black hair is back in a loose ponytail, and he's wearing a shark-tooth necklace.

He looks super bohemian—and super not my type.

But he's fun, he's free, and he was all about going out for a good time. And I know more than anything this week, that's what I need. From the Monticello debacle to the whole Cash thing—the thing that isn't a thing, I remind myself—I need to get away from all this.

"Drinks, then dancing," I say. "Martini to start, please."

He kisses my hand in what's supposed to be a suave move, and it's kind of cute. But in truth, I'm not feeling it. I sigh, leaning on the bar, glancing out at the dance floor. I'm hoping to get my head in the game. Maybe this was a bad idea after all. Maybe I should've gone to the warehouse tonight and worked on inventory. Or maybe I should've stayed home with the cats. But it's too late. I might as well see this whole thing through with Steven.

A new song comes on, and apparently the crowd isn't digging it because there's a mass exodus. Steven orders our drinks behind me, and I'm staring at the dance floor that's now almost empty. Except right in the middle are two people.

Cash Creed, his hands wandering over a tall, tight, tan brunette whose skirt is so short, it could probably count for underwear. They're basically eating each other alive, their kiss so steamy even I'm blushing. She pulls back and giggles wildly, pawing at his chest. They start dancing, her moves definitely stripper inspired. I shake my head. Unreal. So unreal.

"Hey, here's your drink," a voice murmurs in my ear. I jump, forgetting that Steven is with me. I can't take my eyes off Cash Creed, who is smiling that gorgeous smile at her, who is murmuring in her ear. He's probably saying all the things he said to me. And

I don't know why, but it pisses me off. Royally pisses me off.

Just last night, he was teasing me with those eyes, bringing my cat back like some sweet hero in a romance novel. Now, he's here with another woman, clutching onto her like she's his everything. Thank God I didn't invite him to stay. Thank God I'm moving on. But dammit, my blood is boiling. The sight of him with her—it just infuriates me.

"Be right back," I say sweetly to Steven, turning to look at him. He looks confused. Hell, I'm confused. What right do I have to be pissed? I'm here doing the same thing. But I'm not hanging all over Steven... yet. God, this is enraging. This is why I don't get seriously involved. This is exactly why I keep things simple. I'm starting to sound like an insane, desperate, clingy woman with a man who isn't even mine.

No matter how much I tell myself to just slow down, take a breath, I can't seem to stop my stilettos from marching out onto the dance floor. I have no plan for once in my life, and I've got no time to think about it. Before I know it, I'm tapping Cash Creed on the shoulder, his date of the night turning to eye me. I smile at her.

"Hi, how are you?" I ask. *Wow, Sage, great one. Great plan.*

"Sage, hi, how are you? How's Monticello?" He grins at me like I'm some acquaintance he's so happy to meet.

"He's great. What are you doing here? Who's this?" I ask, like I have a right to know. The brunette twirls her ponytail like some high school cheerleader. The only way it would be more fitting is if she were loudly cracking her bubblegum.

"Oh, this is Prudence," Cash says.

"Hi, I'm Prudence," she announces. I smile weakly back. She keeps twirling her hair. I'm pretty sure she's about twenty-two going on thirteen. Seriously.

"So," I say.

"So, is that lonely looking hippie guy in the corner your date tonight?" he asks, and I turn to see Steven standing with his hands in his pockets by an empty table, our drinks sitting on it. He's staring like a lost puppy. For some reason, it makes me sad.

"Yeah, we're here for a good time."

"Well, so are we. Want to join us on the dance floor?"

I stare at him, disbelieving of what I've just heard. What, we're going to bump and grind, the four of us in some odd little date?

"Um, we're good, thanks," I say. "I should probably get going."

At that, the music turns to a slow song. Prudence wraps her arms around Cash, pulling him in. She barely waits until I'm turned around to shove her tongue down his throat. I sidestep so I'm not coated in what I'm imagining to be a waterfall of saliva. Disgusting.

"Shall we?" a voice asks. I turn and bump into Steven, who is apparently ninja-like in his ability to cross a dance floor.

"Um, well," I say, wanting far away from the scene. But, before I can interrupt, he's pulling me in close, his hands sliding down to my hips, his forehead pressed against mine. Wow, this got intimate fast, even for me.

Usually, I'd be feeling it. After all, I came here to forget, to have fun, to have a good night. Swaying to this sappy song, though, this close to Steven, a man I barely know, I'm not feeling good or like this is fun. I actually feel kind of sweaty. About two feet from us, Prudence and Cash are practically making love on the dance floor, their bodies all intertwined. Okay, it's not really that bad. But out of my peripheral, it seems that way.

I pull back from Steven a little bit, and he leans in to kiss my neck. It's not sexy. He doesn't find the right spot, not like....

I find myself turning to eye Cash. Prudence has her

head on his chest now, the lovemaking dance at least temporarily halted. He catches my eye, Steven still doing God knows what to my neck. He winks at me, and my heart flutters. It's just a damn wink. It means nothing. He's just toying with me.

Still, it does something to me. Suddenly, I wish I hadn't let my pride and stubbornness get in the way. I wish I was Prudence, my head on his firm chest, his big, warm hands wrapped around my waist, pulling me in.

"Want to get out of here?" Steven whispers in my ear.

"Um," I say, staring into Steven's eyes now, begging myself to feel something. To forget about Cash, to let that whole scenario go.

But I can't.

Dammit, I can't.

"I'm sorry, Steven. I'm not feeling it."

"Really? You drag me out here, and you're not feeling it?" Steven's getting sort of angry now. "Fine," he says, storming out.

And before I can even mutter a response, he's gone, heading to the exit. I think about going after him, but I really don't want to. Now I'm standing alone under the sad, disco-like lights, the sappy song coming to an end. Cash and Prudence are making out, and I'm standing alone, as it should be.

I skulk off the dance floor, heading to claim my martini. I toss it back and head out the door into the night air to wait for an Uber and to think about how sad the state of my life is.

I really should've just stayed home with the damn cats.

"HEY, THERE SHE IS," HIS VOICE ECHOES FROM THE front office as I wander into the rescue on the following Sunday. I'm wearing sunglasses to hide the bags under my eyes, bags partially caused by the bottle of champagne I polished off last night and partially from tossing and turning wondering why I've lost my game. The champagne, just to be clear, was a purely desperate move. It's been a shitty week of work, of disappointing attempts to get some action, and of thinking over and over about Cash. I got home last night after a sad night out with Harper and wanted to drown my sorrows—but since I only had champagne on hand, it made it even more depressing. Champagne is not the go-to when you're drinking because you feel like shit. It only makes you feel worse because it feels like you're celebrating your sadness.

"Hey," I say, leaving the sunglasses on as I try not to look at his perfectly fitting jeans, the cute shirt he's wearing. I try not to think about how the huge smile on his face probably has something to do with Prudence. And I try to remind myself that I really don't care if it does.

"So, looks like you and Steven didn't really have a great night the other night, huh?"

At this, I shove the sunglasses back on my head. "And why do you care?" My voice comes out a little edgier than I wanted. Janice is sweeping up nearby. She looks at me before hurrying into the other section, giving us our privacy apparently.

He puts his hands up, grinning. "I'm just saying. Seems like you left on a sour note."

"Well, we did. Not everyone just gives it up to anyone, you know. I wasn't feeling it." I head behind the desk, busying my hands with filing, trying to pretend I'm ignoring him. He leans on the counter.

"Well, if it matters, I think Steve-o looked like a weirdo. You may have dodged a bullet there."

I glare at him. "Oh, and your preppy little Prudence looked so much better."

"She was interesting. I mean, I won't lie, her voice,

super annoying. But, she's got this really cool thing she can do with her—"

"Enough," I shout, hands up. He just laughs.

"Why are you so edgy?"

"I'm not edgy. I just don't need to hear about your sexcapades with Prudence."

"So now you're conservative about sex? After you fucked me and ran?" he asks, his eyes still teasing.

"Oh my God, keep your voice down. The whole shelter doesn't need to hear about that." I glance around to see where Janice is.

He laughs. "You're crazy. But listen, if you were jealous and wanted to explore a sexcapade, as you call it, with me the other night, you should've said something. I'd have sent Prudence off with Steven."

"Okay, first, you're a dick. And two, I was *not* jealous of you. Give me a break." I roll my eyes and head over to the copy machine to make a few copies from yesterday's adoptions before I head back to the cat room.

This guy is unreal. So arrogant. What the hell was I thinking? Clearly he's full of himself, way too full of himself.

But before I can push the green button on the copier, I feel breathing on my neck, hands on my waist. I think about jerking away, but then there's a soft kiss planted on my neck. And, unlike Steven the other night, he knows exactly the spot.

I bite my lip as he nibbles my ear, leaning in to whisper. "Well, I'll tell you a secret. When I was dancing with Prudence, I kept hoping you'd come over and ask me to dance. I kept hoping you'd ask me to be with you. Because I would've said yes, Sage. I want to say yes. You make me crazy."

My heart is beating so wildly, I'm certain he can hear it. I take a deep breath, relishing in the feel of his strong body against mine.

And then a barking dog brings me to my senses. I shrug him off me. "Well, this would never work. You know that. Besides, I'm not interested in a relationship."

I feel the ice queen coming back. I shove aside the beating heart, the warmth he brought to my veins. I try to exit the room, heading to the cat room before he makes me lose my mind. He spins me around in his arms, though, and forces me to look at him.

"You know, I get it. I do. Because I really don't believe in anything but sex. But you have to admit it, Sage Everling, when we're around each other, sparks fly. And it's more than just sexual sparks. There's just... something there. I think maybe we've each met our match, and I don't know, it kind of excites me. Maybe we should set aside our rules and play this thing out, just one more time. See what happens."

I look up into those dark, brooding eyes, and I think about saying yes. I think about what it would be like to climb back into bed with him. I think about Monday night, in Steven's arms, how much I wanted to be in Cash's.

I sigh. "I don't think so. Look, I won't lie. You intrigue me. More than I'd like to admit. But you're also dangerous. I don't like to be beat at my own game."

"So you admit I could beat you," he says, smirking.

"Dream on. But I just think the two of us together would be like playing with fire. It would never work. We don't want it to work."

He leans in now so close I think he's going to kiss me. "I've never been one to shy away from fire."

We lock eyes, a long moment passing between us. "Me neither. But for right now, I don't think we can take the risk." I brush past him into the cat room, my heart still beating wildly as I parade into the area, knowing he's staring at me go.

I'm not afraid of fire... but I'm sure as hell afraid of the fire Cash Creed has stirred in me. And for the first time in my life, I have no clue what I'm doing.

SIXTEEN

Cash

———

"OH MY GOD, I CAN'T BELIEVE YOU PICKED THAT ONE," Jodie squeals as I wink at her, slapping the highly inappropriate card on the table.

"Oh please, after the one you just picked about blow jobs? Come on, you can't pretend to be all innocent now," I reply, shaking my head as Avery laughs so hard I think she might burst.

"Another point for me," Reed says, grabbing at the card, smiling in delight as he pats the stack in front of him. "Guys, this game is so easy. You just have to know how to read people. I know what makes Cash laugh."

"Oh, do you?" Lysander asks, teasing. "What have you two been up to when I'm not around?"

Levi gets up for another round of beers. We're all crammed into Jodie and Levi's townhouse for a night of cards and drinking. I laugh as Jesse flips the next fill-in-the-blank card, and I examine my hand.

"Oh, please. He's too busy pining over the Everling girl to do anything with anyone," Jodie teases.

"So how are things in that department? Details, details," Reed says as he puts a white card facedown in the pile in front of Jesse, offering a wink as he does.

"How does this always become the topic?" I ask, shaking my head.

"Because we're all eternally hooked. We can't appreciate the chase anymore, so we have to do it through you," Lysander replies pointedly.

"Yeah, if you didn't want us prodding you about your sex life, you should've found a group of wily singles," Avery replies.

I sigh. "Well, things are going... pretty okay. I think I'm winning her over."

There is a collective pause. "Wait, you mean you might be in a real relationship?" Levi asks, mocking a heart attack.

"Don't get ahead of yourself," I reply, pretending to study my cards. "It's just, well, I think there might be something else here. And I think I might be on the verge of convincing her to give it a try. She's a tough one to crack."

"And you're not?" Reed asks, smirking.

"Do you think she could be the one?" Avery asks softly, and I look up at her. I bite my lip, wondering how much to divulge.

"You all know I don't roll like that."

"But maybe with this one, you do," Jodie adds matter-of-factly.

I pause, taking a deep breath. I can't deny there's something special there. Sure, she's hot as hell and the sex was out of this world. But as I told Sage yesterday, it's more than that. There's something. There's certainly something that makes me wonder if maybe we could be playing for keeps instead of playing for one night or two.

"You know, there is a party over at the Marooned Pirate tomorrow night. I bet Sage will be there. Sounds like a good time and all," Reed adds.

"Oh, stop. You just want an excuse to go to the party tomorrow," Lysander chides.

"When did I ever need an excuse?" Reed asks before lifting his beer and taking a sip. "But seriously, scope it out. Tell her how you really feel. We'll all come for support to cheer you on."

I eye the whole table, shaking my head. "And you think that's how I win over Sage Everling? A cheering squad?"

"Well, we're not just any cheering squad, to be fair.

I mean, look at us," Levi says, tipping his hat in the gesture he knows annoys me.

"I don't know. She's probably going to be there with someone. I don't want to scare her off either. I've been coming on strong lately."

"And strong seems to be her vice, if you ask me," Avery replies. "Come on. Stop being a wuss and just go for it."

"To going for it," Reed says, raising his bottle. The whole crew joins in, clicking bottles as I sigh.

Even though I don't say it out loud, maybe they're right. Maybe I need to just go for it, see where this thing leads. Maybe all Sage needs, all she wants is for me to take the reins and take charge.

SEVENTEEN

Cash

———

"You do know she might not be here?" I ask as we get out of the limo Reed rented—he insisted we had to arrive at the party in style because it was such a big night. I still think he's just aiming for an Evermore bag. The man doesn't give up.

"She'll be here. I feel it in my bones. Plus, I didn't put on this Evermore tie for nothing," Reed replies, leading us all into the Marooned Pirate like a sad posse.

"Please, can we all just act natural? I don't want her feeling like we're preying on her," I say, a little nervous now that bringing the crew was a terrible idea. In truth, though, I didn't bring them—they drug me here, insisting it'll all be good.

"When do we ever not act natural?" Levi asks, messing up my hair.

"Is that a serious question?" I ask, smirking. I do love their enthusiasm, and, in reality, I know that this is just an excuse for them all to come out and party hard.

Still, I can't help but feel like a nerdy, awkward boy walking into senior prom alone. This girl's got me off my game. I keep thinking about what could go wrong or about how I'm going to make this work. What if she's adamant about not giving this a chance? What if she's not here, or what if she is—with someone else? And why do I care so much? Jesus, I either need to make it work with Sage, or I seriously need to get laid. This adrenaline is too much.

We saunter up to the bar, the seven of us taking up an entire side. Lysander starts ordering drinks, knowing our usuals, as I scan the bar. It's packed in here, with two-dollar margaritas and a hot local band flooding the place with more than just the regulars. However, as I scan the dance floor, my heart stops.

In a tiny black dress barely long enough to cover anything, she's dancing in the middle of the floor. But she is, of course, not alone. A tall, lanky guy in a button-up shirt with the sleeves rolled up is all over her, preying on her. He's basically laying claim to her, which is discernible from even back here.

"Shit," I mutter, and Jodie leans over my shoulder to see what I'm saying.

"You knew this might happen, right? So don't sweat it. You also know she's not serious about him, right? He's a rebound. She's just telling herself her old ways are still okay. It's fine, Cash. Go tell her how you feel."

"I already have. Jodie, this is ridiculous. She's made it clear what she's all about. I need to let it go."

"And you've also made it clear you can't do that. And from what you've told me, she can't either. Now come on. Buck up, bronco. Get your A-game on and get the hell out there. Go show her what she's missing."

Reed slaps a shot in my hand, and the crew cheers me on. I down the shot. Lysander hands me another, as does Levi. Three shots down, a slap on the back from my brother, and I know what I have to do.

EIGHTEEN

Sage

———

"LET ME SHOW YOU MY MOVES. YOU'RE GOING TO DIG them," Carl whispers in my ear. Instead of giving me chills, it gives me the creeps. Still, I down my fifth margarita—at two dollars, who can pass them up?—and follow him to the floor.

Coming here was a mistake. I knew it from the moment I agreed to let Carl Jacobson, the man behind me in line for coffee yesterday, take me to the Marooned Pirate Summer Bash. Still, he's a business owner himself, confident, and looking for fun. Even though my gut told me to stay home and focus on work, my heart told me to get back out there and let Carl push this crazy Cash Creed business out of my mind.

Because since Sunday, since the breathless

moment at the shelter, I can't get the damn Texan off my mind. I'm making pancakes, thinking about the feel of his hands on my body. I'm sitting with Monticello, imagining him in those tight jeans, thinking about how sweet he is with all of the dogs at the shelter. I'm hearing his laugh, thinking about his witty comebacks, and wishing he was here looking at me like he does. I'm thinking about all of the things we have in common, and all the things I don't yet know about him but want to.

Shit, I'm toast.

So maybe that's why I said yes to the lanky, tall business exec yesterday—and to the multiple margaritas. Maybe that's why I've been able to ignore the fact that Carl pronounces way too many words wrong and spits when he talks. I've ignored the fact that he laughs way too loudly at his own cheesy puns—there are a lot of them, to be clear—and how he insists that he could help me make Evermore even more profitable.

Gag me.

But five margaritas in, and I'm being drug to the dance floor, knowing this date is going nowhere... even more than normal. As in, it's not even heading toward a one-night stand. I should just politely leave, head home to my sofa and the cats, and mourn the status of my sad, lone heart. Still, I know deep down there's a reason I haven't just yet. And, as Carl gyrates his hips in a weirdly unsatisfying way, I glance to my right and see the exact reason out of my peripheral.

Cash Creed. He's here.

The flutter in my chest is undeniable. The flame in my heart is unquenchable. He's here, and suddenly Carl melts away. I ignore his pelvic thrusts that are way too weird and close for comfort, my eyes landing on the man in the sexy suit jacket and tight jeans who is strutting my way.

Dammit, I'm a goner... but studying him as he comes closer, I tell myself it could be worse. So much worse. And I tell myself that maybe, just maybe, Sage Everling is ready to take the risk.

***

"Hey, there," he says when he gets close to me.

"Excuse me," I say to Carl, who seemingly doesn't care that I'm gone, feeling way too into his dancing groove to stop. He keeps up the wonky moves even when I've stepped several feet away from him, close enough to Cash to smell his cologne.

"Hey," I reply back, wondering where the confident Cash and Sage have gone. We're both standing here, dancing around our words cautiously like two awkward teenagers.

"Look," I say right when he says "Listen."

"Go ahead," I murmur.

"No, you go ahead," he replies.

For two people who like to take the lead, we're failing miserably.

Cash finally takes the lead, jumping into his statement. "Okay, fuck it. Here goes nothing. I like you. A lot. And I know we both have our rules and our stipulations, and I respect that. I do. But dammit, I am sick of trying to get you out of my head and trying to find someone to replace this burning sensation in my chest when I see you. I don't know if this could work with us. I know it probably won't. But I just want to... I need to get to know you, to see what we could be."

I open my mouth to respond—with what, I don't have time to figure out—because as my mouth opens, Cash steps forward, bridging the gap between us. With a pumping song blasting on the dance floor and sweaty people all around us, Cash grabs my face and presses his lips into mine. Quickly, the kiss turns hungry, and he claims my mouth with his, our tongues swirling in a starving rhythm of need, lust, passion, and everything else the heart speaks to.

When we finally pull back, I'm in a daze, staring

into the dark eyes of the man who has torn down walls I thought were permanently cemented in place.

"Do you want to get out of here, go somewhere?" he asks, his voice paradoxically strong and breathy.

I raise an eyebrow. "Like... do you mean...." I ask, wondering if we're floating back into one-night or two-night stand territory.

He blinks for a few seconds. "No, I actually think I mean let's go somewhere to talk, to spend time together. You know, in a conventional, dating sort of sense. Wow, I really do think I mean that," he says, as if surprised by his own confession.

"Sounds great," I say. Cash grabs my hand but before we can leave the dance floor, there's a tapping on my shoulder. I know who it is before I even turn around. Shit. Carl. I forgot all about him.

"So, does this mean you're not coming back to my place?" he asks, a sad look on his face.

I choose kindness. "I'm so sorry. Something's come up. Thank you for a lovely time," I lie. Carl raises an eyebrow, the lanky businessman now standing and staring at us both.

"Well, you know what, it's fine. But before you go...."

And before I can even blink, he's planting a fist into Cash Creed's beautiful face. My mouth falls open in shock, Cash stumbling backward as people scream around us. In a moment, Cash's brother is over, looking for Carl, but Carl is long gone.

"Shit," Cash murmurs, holding his nose.

"I'm so sorry," I reply, rushing over to see how much damage there is.

"Do you want me to go after him?" Levi asks, puffing his chest, the redhead hanging on his arm.

"It's fine. I'm fine," Cash says, looking more embarrassed than anything. He pulls his hands back from his face to reveal a bloody mess.

"Oh shit, we should get you to the hospital," I reply, panic setting in.

"I'm fine. I'm totally fine," he says.

Before we can even talk about it more, a man rushes over with a towel and some ice from the bar. "Coming through," the man says. "I've seen my share of bar fights. Come on. Let's get you to a booth and get you cleaned up."

Levi and the man with ice rush Cash to the corner booth to stop the bleeding. I take a deep breath, wondering if this is a sign of what a disaster Cash and I will be together.

"Oh, darling, aren't you just a ball of excitement?" a man says, handing me a margarita. "Reed Wyatt, a pleasure to meet you." I smile, noticing his tie, as I take the margarita and head toward the table.

"I feel like I should be doing something."

Reed waves me off. "My hubby has it under control. Trust me, a man like Cash can handle a few fists. He might look all pretty boy, but those Creeds are Texan tough. And I know for a fact he's not going to let anything slow him down after winning your hand."

I smile, liking him already. "So have you known Cash long?" I ask.

Reed takes a sip of his own margarita before replying. "Long enough to know he's a keeper. Sure, he's got some walls up when it comes to love. But, darling, that man is a handful. And something tells me a woman like you needs a man who can keep it exciting, no?"

I smile, feeling my stomach settle down as I see that Cash is already looking better, refusing to hold ice on his face despite Lysander and Levi fighting with him.

"You're right in that respect. Nice tie, by the way," I reply, smiling.

"So, you know, I've heard a few things about these Evermore bags coming out...."

I grin, knowing where this is all going—and for once, feeling like it's going to be more than okay.

"I'M SO SORRY AGAIN. I HAD NO IDEA LANKY CARL HAD A swing like that," I say as Cash holds my hand, leading me out of the bar.

"I'm fine. Really. I mean, I think it makes me look a little badass to tell you the truth," Cash replies, looking at me. Luckily, his nose isn't broken—Carl's punch isn't that great, thankfully. But he's going to have some bruising, and the swelling is already making me reconsider whether we should be going to the hospital. He has insisted he's fine—and all the men in his friend circle assured the same thing.

"It does make you look rugged," I reply, leaning into him, feeling inexplicably giggly.

"I'm the one who should be apologizing. Jodie told me that Reed wrangled a bag out of you," he says.

I shrug. "It's fine. Seriously. The least I could do."

"You do know you'll get some great promo from that bag. Reed will be toting that thing everywhere. It's all I've heard about since talking about you."

I raise an eyebrow. "So you talk about me?"

He pauses our walking for a second. "You know, a little."

"And what do you say?"

"Good stuff, of course."

"Uh huh."

He looks at me as we stop, the moonlight illuminating his face. "What bad is there to say? You're sexy, smart, sophisticated, and a whole lot of fun."

"You barely know me," I reply honestly, not breaking our gaze.

"So let's change that," he says.

"Isn't that what we're doing?"

"Well, then let's get on with it."

"So, where do you want to go?" I ask, and we pause, thinking. The truth is, for as many people as we've been out with, neither of us has really done the traditional dating thing. How is this thing done? I wish Harper had come out tonight—she had a cake tasting to go to—so I could have gotten some last second advice.

"How about the beach?" he asks, shrugging.

"Now? It's dark."

"Perfect timing. No sunscreen required, and all the shrieking families will be asleep. This is *the* time to hit the sand."

"But we're all dressed up," I reply, looking down at my outfit.

"Well, let me think. I do believe one of us owns her own fashion house, so I'm pretty sure there's more where that came from. But you know, if you're worried, you could always strip down, leave it behind on the boardwalk for safe keeping."

I grin, hitting his arm. "That's not how this getting to know you thing is supposed to work. We already know those parts of each other."

"Hey, I'm just looking out for you. And your fancy dress," he says, putting his hands up.

I smile as we walk on, ambling toward the boardwalk and then finally the sand. I kick off my heels and leave them on a bench, the ocean breeze whipping my hair out of my face and making it a frizzy mess. Still, I don't care. I breathe in the salty scent as Cash pulls me toward the water.

"You do know this is probably not recommended. It's dangerous down here at this time of night. People drown."

He smirks.

"What? I'm serious," I say.

"You don't strike me as the type who is afraid of danger," he replies.

I shrug. "I'm afraid of some things, for sure."

"Like what?"

"Failure."

"You? Are you serious?"

I turn and study him. "We all have our insecurities.

Evermore wasn't always a sure thing. It still isn't. Things change. People change."

"But isn't that the fun of it? Never knowing when things will change?" he asks, closing the gap between us as we stand on the sand, above the rising tide. He pushes a strand of hair out of my eyes, and my body reacts to the touch of his skin on mine.

"I'm learning that sometimes change is necessary. But I guess I'm also afraid of trusting too much. I've been burned a lot in the past. Not just romantically, either. By family. By those who were supposed to stand by me."

I don't know if it's his dark eyes or the stars or the fact I haven't been out here on the sand in so long, but I chide myself for being so vulnerable. Why am I opening up so much? This isn't like me. Still, Cash stares at me, stares into me, like he gets it. For the first time in my life, I feel like someone truly gets it.

"Well, sometimes, I guess we just have to face up to our fears and learn to run with it. What do you say?" His voice is almost a whisper, and for a moment, I see the other side of Cash Creed, the one hiding behind the playboy. I see this serious, soft side that overflows with empathy, with loyalty, with love.

This time, I am the one to initiate our kiss. This one, though, lacks the hungry, prey-like consumption of the kiss on the dance floor. This kiss is soft and gentle, an opening up of two people who haven't done this before—this vulnerability thing.

When he pulls back, he looks down into my face, his hands cupping my chin. "Look, I'm scared too. Of the same things as you. But maybe, I don't know, we can help each other realize that trusting people isn't always bad, and failure isn't a life-ruiner. Let's cut ourselves some slack. Let's see what we could do together, because you know what, I think we might surprise ourselves."

And, with the salty air still whipping around us, the sound of the crashing waves to our side, I nod, knowing that the Sage Everling who walked onto this sand is a little bit different than the one walking off.

NINETEEN

Cash

<hr>

"Surprise," I say, holding a coffee and a bag from the Pancake House down the street. For a split second, I wonder if she's going to toss me out. Instead, she smiles.

"What's this?" she asks, standing in sweatpants and a T-shirt, her hair up in a messy bun.

"Breakfast."

It's Sunday morning, an hour before we start our work at the shelter. I couldn't resist sneaking in some extra time with Sage. We've gone for coffee one evening this week, and she swung by Midsummer Nights for a breakfast meeting the other day. But we didn't go home together on any of those occasions, not even the night after those steamy beach kisses.

In fact, we've both set new ground rules, ones that

neither of us are familiar with. No sex. No steamy nights. Just normal, average dating. And although I'm enjoying getting to know her, I have to say this—it sucks. The lust is getting harder and harder to ignore, and when she turns to lead me into her kitchen, the way her sweatpants cling to her ass makes it even harder to forget the fact I wasn't cut out for this. I must have a penchant for torture to agree to this.

Two cats come crying from the living room, one the familiar hairless who I sort of owe for helping me win over Sage.

"Sorry, the place is kind of a mess. Launch is coming up, so there are samples everywhere," she apologizes as she leads me to the kitchen island that also serves as a bar with stools. I glance around at fabrics, accessories, and even clothing strewn about. It's chaotic but exciting, just like Sage.

"So what's in the bag?" she asks, grinning, as she takes a seat beside me.

"Well, I remembered that you like pancakes, so that's what I went with. I'm a terrible cook, in truth, so I let someone else make them. Hope you don't mind."

"Are you kidding? These are my favorites. Don't tell Lysander, of course. The pancakes at Midsummer are good, too."

"Trust me, I'm not confessing that I went somewhere else for breakfast today," I grin, pulling out the platters as we sit down to eat.

We both dig in, chatting about mundane things like the weather and the news—none of which feels mundane sitting beside the sexy blonde. After a few minutes of conversation, though, she pauses and stares at me, grinning.

"What?"

"Is this the first time you've had breakfast with a woman without having sex the night before?"

I grin right back. "Got me there. Hell, I think this might be the first time I've had breakfast with a woman."

"Stop it," she says, shaking her head. "Really?"

"You know my rules," I tease.

"Quite a different set of rules these days," she says, and I wonder if I should take the lead to open up the conversation about what we're doing here, about what we are.

I don't. That's a complication to deal with another time. For now, I'm just sitting back and enjoying this ride with a beautiful woman who makes me hot in all the right ways and settled in all the other right ways.

After we finish breakfast, Sage smiles. "Thanks. I could get used to this."

"I'm sort of counting on that," I reply.

"Are you?" she asks.

I stare at the woman who is wearing sweatpants and a T-shirt but making my heart race faster than any woman ever has. "Yeah, I think I am."

"Good," she replies before leaning down to pet Monticello and Barcelona.

"Your car or mine?" she asks, and I grin.

"Do you have to ask? No way I'm letting you drive me. Come on, a player has to hang on to some aspects of his masculinity."

"I could say so much to that, but I won't because I'm too tired to deal with the traffic anyway. Your car it is," she says, grabbing her bag as we head down to my car, off to a day of barking dogs and meowing cats— and to keep exploring this thing between us.

TWENTY

Sage

"Holy crap, I never thought I'd see this day again," Harper says, sticking the spoon in the bubbling baked beans on the stove. "These are actually delish. Are they a Pinterest recipe?"

I grin. "Those are from a can. Hey, I couldn't pull off everything from scratch."

"I still can't believe it. A few weeks out from a launch, and you're usually nothing but work. And now you're taking off a whole night to cook dinner for a man at your place? Honestly, I feel like I'm in an episode of *Black Mirror*."

I pull the cornbread out of the oven as I turn to her. "I thought you'd be ecstatic."

"Oh, I am," she says, putting her hands up in the

air. "I am thoroughly overjoyed that Sage Everling is not only putting down work, but she's giving a man a chance at more than one night. I just never thought I'd see the day. What changed?"

For a moment I turn to her, serious, oven mitts on my hands. "I don't know. I think it's just... him. I can't explain it."

Harper lets out a squeal, and I almost regret the serious moment. "Oh, he's it then. I had the same feeling with Brad. The same inexplicable feeling. Oh Jesus, you're going to marry a Texan. How exciting!"

"Okay, slow down. This is nothing like you and Brad. You've always been a hopeless romantic. Me, not so much. This is still new to me, and to be honest, I might not like it. I might give this a go for a few weeks and decide it's too much."

"Stop it. You're a goner and you know it. I've never seen you smile so much."

I smile, to my chagrin, at this statement. "I know. God, is this what it feels like?"

"Is this what what feels like?"

"Love."

After the word is out of my mouth, I'm kind of in shock. Who am I, throwing that word around again? But dammit, I can't deny that he does something to me, that he makes me feel all sorts of things I didn't think were possible.

"Well, let's see, cooking a five-course Texan feast almost from scratch for a man? Yeah, it might be love. Or you're pregnant and craving spicy foods. Are you pregnant?"

"No," I reply harshly, shaking my head vehemently. "Absolutely not."

"Okay, then it's love. Where'd you get all these food ideas from?" she asks, flipping the ribs in the oven while I tend to the dessert.

"I chatted with Levi about it yesterday. He tipped me off."

"Getting in with the family, too. Wow, Sage, you're doing this dating thing like a pro."

I sigh.

"What is it now?" she asks, rolling her eyes. "You really are like a naïve sixteen-year-old when it comes to this thing."

"I don't know. We just haven't really talked about what this is officially. Are we exclusive? Are we serious? I don't know."

"Time will tell. But honey, the way he looks at you, trust me. He's not going anywhere. He's in it for real. I've known since the first time I chatted with him."

I'm putting the finishing touches on the cheesecake—not so Texan, but apparently Cash has a thing for cheesecake—when it dawns on me.

"Wait a second, did you say since you chatted with him?"

"Oh, shit. That's right. I never brought that one up. Yeah, not long after you met him, I ran into him at the dog park. He didn't know who I was, but I scoped him out. I knew from that second on he was a keeper, that he was perfect for you."

"Why didn't you say something?"

She shrugs. "Would you have listened?"

I weigh her words. "No, probably not."

"Exactly. Sometimes, it's better to silently plant the seed."

"What does that mean?"

"Oh, nothing. But listen, when the wedding comes along, is it okay for me to tell that story about you in Panera Bread, or no? You know, for my speech? I need to start drafting this thing because you know I'm a terrible writer."

"Oh, look at that. I think it might be time for you to head home," I tease. "Don't you have some designs to work on?"

"And don't you have a ton of marketing to work on? I mean, if the boss is taking some time to play, I think a lowly employee can do the same. Me and Brad are going to get busy tonight."

"First, you're not a lowly employee. You're the heart of this company. And two, I didn't need that mental image. Now get out of here. Take a few pieces of cornbread with you."

Harper grins. "Am I your guinea pig now? What, if we don't choke and die on this stuff, then it'll be okay for Cash?"

"You've got it. So send me a text after you eat it to tell me you lived."

"We might be too busy for a text," she teases, laying into the word "busy" heavily.

"I love you," I shout after swatting her away. She heads toward the door, stooping down to pet Barcelona goodbye.

"Love you back. Now wrangle that cowboy," she says.

"He's not a cowboy. Far from it."

"Closest you'll ever get, probably, so own it. Good luck tonight."

"You too," I shout.

She peeks back through the almost-shut door. "I don't need luck to get lucky anymore."

Before I can spout something back, the door slams, and I'm alone to finish dinner, finish my makeup, and finish owning the fact Cash Creed's coming over, breaking even more rules I've set out for myself.

Then again, I'm pretty sure the entire book of rules has been chucked out at this point. I guess that's the thing about lust and love and whatever the hell this is. Sometimes it changes the rules for you, and you just have to learn how to play all over again.

TWENTY-ONE

Cash

———

"So, how was dinner last night? Did Sage's cooking hold up to Mama's?" Levi asks as I lean back in the desk chair at the apartment complex. Levi's swung by to go over some business issues with me, but also to interrogate me about last night. I wouldn't expect any less.

"Yeah, it was pretty damn good," I reply, grinning as I lace my fingers behind my head, kicking my feet up on the desk.

"Wait until Mama hears. Have you talked to her lately? Because she has been on my case about you. Wondering how you're doing, if you're behaving, and if there's a woman in the picture."

"Please tell me you didn't tell her about Sage," I reply.

Levi grins. "How much is the secret worth to you?"

"More than I have. Jesus, if that woman hears a hint of me getting serious, she'll be down here buying mother-of-the-bride dresses and giving Sage Grandma's ring before I can even blink."

"And would that be such a bad thing?"

"Ditto, brother. You're in a serious relationship. Why don't you give Grandma's ring a hand to rest on?"

"You know that's not mine and Jodie's thing," Levi replies.

"Then it sure as hell isn't mine and Sage's."

"We'll see."

"Anyway," I say, trying to shift the subject.

"Anyway, was the after-dinner activity just as good?" Levi winks, and I roll my eyes.

"Don't worry about my after-dinner activities, brother. You know I'm a pro in those respects."

"That's why I was surprised you wanted to meet here so early."

"I didn't spend the night last night."

Levi's jaw drops. "You're kidding."

"I'm not. We're doing things a little differently."

"So you sex her up, then get to know her? You go fast and then slow?"

"It's all about timing, Levi. You should know that. And yes, we've decided to try a different approach."

"How's that working for you?"

I think about lying. But hell, Levi knows me better than anyone. "Honestly? I wanted nothing more than to say fuck our new rules and shred that sexy dress she was wearing off with my teeth. But you know, I am patient when I need to be."

"We'll see how long this lasts."

"I guess we will. Now, can we get serious for a minute?"

"Shoot." Levi readjusts his hat.

I sigh, standing up from the chair. I'm not one to admit defeat, so this isn't easy.

"Well, things are a tad bit off around here."

"As in...?" Levi asks, walking toward me.

"As in we've had an uptick in tenant complaints. About facilities breaking, about some of the renters, and maybe about the fact I forgot to check the voice-mail for Grandad's phone number and there were about twenty unanswered issues."

"Are you serious, Cash?"

"I'm serious," I admit. I sigh. "Look, in my defense, I told you I wasn't cut out for this."

"And I told you I needed you to be. Cash, you know things are crazy with Jodie's writing and with Wild Hearts. I thought you said you had it under control."

"I thought I did. But I guess running this place and all the other rentals is harder than I thought. I just, I wanted you to be aware so I don't leave you with a shit-storm on your hands. Thought you could help me get a handle on it so it'll be easier when I have to pass it off."

Levi blinks, tilting his head. "Pass it off? What do you mean?"

Now it's my turn to be surprised. I lean in on the paper-covered desk. "I mean at the end of summer, when I go home."

There is a lengthy pause.

"What?" I ask when Levi just continues to stare, looking like he's seen the ghost of Grandpa.

"I just.... Wow. I just thought with all this Sage stuff and how you were fitting in with all of our crew, I don't know, Cash. I just thought maybe you were fixing to settle in here."

I laugh, shaking my head. "What? Me? Settling down? Levi, hold up. I told you at the beginning of all this that I was staying temporarily. This is your gig, not mine."

Levi crosses his arms. "But what's back in Texas for you? Some hours in the law offices with Mom and Dad, doing the same thing every day? Screwing the same women over and over and yet feeling lonely? I don't know, Cash. I just thought maybe you were building something here that you'd want to hang on to."

"Dammit, Levi," I say, my temper flaring. "I told you when I took this not to get used to me being here, that it was for a short period of time. This isn't me. What, you think doing a half-assed job running rental properties is what I imagined for myself? It's been fun, real fun. But I never planned on staying here. This is your dream, buddy. Not mine."

Levi sighs. "I'm sorry. I just, well, it's been nice having you here. I'd hoped that Sage changed your mind."

"You know I don't operate like that. Yeah, Sage and I have something. And hell, it might even turn into a serious something. But you also know I'm the last man in the world to make a decision based on a woman. And I know she's the same. That's why we were both so hesitant to start this whole thing. Look, just because it's moved beyond one night doesn't mean it's anything more than fun."

Levi chuckles now, and I'm pissed again. "What the hell's so funny?"

"Sorry, it's not you, not really. It's just, well, I know another Texan who said the exact same thing not too long ago. And hell, that guy was screwed and didn't even know it. Sometimes, brother, someone comes along and changes everything you thought you knew about yourself. I'm just saying don't be surprised if things shake up differently than you planned."

Before I can refute what he said or get angry or punch him, he's calmly striding across the office to the door.

"Wait up, what about all this tenant shit?"

Levi peeks back in the door. "You're smart, Cash. You'll figure it out. And if you don't, who cares, right? After all, this is all just temporary." He tips his hat like the cocky son-of-a-bitch he sometimes is, grins, and strolls right on out, leaving me to stew at the office window wondering why the thought of settling in here has me so fuming mad.

Or maybe now that I'm alone with my thoughts I can admit a scarier reality—it's not anger I'm feeling.

It's terror.

TWENTY-TWO

Sage

"So, before we get to talking about the upcoming promos and finishing touches on the line and all of that, I have some news," Harper says, her smile spreading on her face as she warms her hands on her cup of tea.

We're out for breakfast this morning, and even though I've barely slept in days with the stress of the upcoming line weighing me down, I feel lighter looking at Harper. I've noticed she's been beaming lately. I assumed it was just because Brad has been keeping her busy and glowing, but now, I step back and realize something else is at play.

"Okay," I say, wanting to let her savor this moment. I can tell her announcement is going to be big.

"We're postponing the wedding."

I blink, not sure if I've heard my friend right. I even lean in, as if getting closer to her will verify that I've misunderstood the already-spoken sentiment.

"Wait, what?"

"The wedding. It's postponed."

I study her smile, still not comprehending. This was just about the last thing on my mind.

"And you're happy about this?"

"Sort of," she says. "I mean, I was looking forward to all of the stuff we had planned, but it will just come later than we thought."

"Okay. Should I be worried?" I ask, sipping my coffee now, wondering if my sleep deprivation is finally catching up.

"Well, no. I don't think so. Um, here's the thing."

There is an epic pause, the kind right before something life changing spews from someone's mouth.

"I'm pregnant."

And with two words, her smile erupts into contagious laughter. I set down my cup, abandoning the caffeine for the surge I get from Harper's joy. We hug in the middle of the café, people looking, but I don't care.

"Harper, congratulations. I can't believe it. I thought you've been glowing, but I just thought it was a whole lot of sex."

"Well, it kind of was. But yeah, we're expecting. And my due date is right around the wedding. So we thought why rush it, you know? We can just have the wedding a year later or something. I don't know. We'll figure it out. It doesn't even matter now, you know?"

We take our seats, and I watch Harper animatedly talk about what a surprise it was but how happy it made her. She talks about how she didn't think she wanted kids until she saw that positive pregnancy test, and how even though this changes everything, she's so excited.

"I'm happy for you," I say, nodding. Studying Harper, I recognize a joy that has felt so distant to me for most of my life. The joy of unconditional connection with another, the joy of knowing your life isn't just about you anymore.

A joy that suddenly makes me feel a little bit sad for my own state of affairs.

I shove it down, though, knowing this moment is Harper's. We spend the morning talking about nurseries and names and pregnancy tips instead of the Evermore release—and I couldn't be happier.

When we part ways and I head back to my home, ready to tackle some of the marketing and final details on my own, giving Harper the rest of the day off to celebrate, I try to shove aside the melancholy that's settling in.

What's wrong with me? I've never been like this before. Never been jealous of others who have the traditional life, the life I claim not to want.

But as I step inside my empty condo, the only sound the meowing of my cats, I study the lifeless walls, the pictureless mantle, and I wonder if I've made the right decision at all.

And most of all, later on when I'm sitting on my balcony alone with my thoughts, I think about the horrible moments that changed my life path, that made me the Sage I am today, and that made me the woman who rejected traditional love in all senses of the word.

I wonder as I sip my lemonade, cracking my flip flop against my heel, if things could've been different for me if that one moment just hadn't happened.

"WHO'S SHEILA?" I ASK MOM POINTEDLY AS SHE'S SIPPING *wine and pulling the pasta dinners from the bag. Dad's on a business trip, and I'm grounded after a minor transgression with my phone and a boy named Steven—long story. At the name, I think Mom's going to spit out her wine. Her* eyes widen, and she stares at me as if I've just summoned a demon.

"Where did you hear the name Sheila?" she asks. I can tell she's trying to regain her composure, her eyebrows knitting together in an inquisitive look. She sets down her wine glass, and I can see her employing the deep breathing techniques from her therapist.

I reach for the takeout bag from the top-notch Italian restaurant across town, meeting her eyes. I didn't expect this kind of reaction. In truth, I was just making conversation. After all, at fourteen, I felt like there were few things I could talk about with my mom or wanted to talk about with my mom.

"Dad was on the phone yesterday when I got home from school. I heard him saying some weird stuff. Not to worry, that it would all be okay, that everyone understood. Then I heard him say Sheila. I figured it was a new secretary or something."

I lift out my meal and pause as Mom looks visibly shaken. She's never been a woman I'd consider strong, but perhaps that's not really fair. Mom and I have always butted heads. I've always despised her lack of drive, how she seems okay just riding on Dad's success and not fretting about building a life, a passion of her own. Now, though, I feel a mixing sense of dread and sorrow fill my chest.

"Mom?"

"She's no one, dear. Now pass the salt."

I freeze, blinking, wondering how everything can be so complicated yet so transparent in this family.

"Mom, answer me. Who is she?"

"Sage, just drop it, will you? Some things aren't for you to know." She raises her voice, and I can see tears starting to well in her eyes. My stomach drops.

"Dammit, Mom, I'm tired of all the secrets in this family. I'm tired of always being on the outside."

"Sage Everling, you will change your tone. Now drop it."

But it's too late. Her composure cracks, the tears fall, and I know instinctively that life's about to shift.

"Mom, just tell me," I murmur, softer, more encouraging.

She meets my eyes, and woman to woman, we connect in a way we haven't before.

"She's your father's mistress."

Hearing the words stabs into me in a way I hadn't expected. I've known since I was young that my parents aren't perfect. Their condescending attitudes, their conniving, manipulative business methods, and their constant judgement of me have me ready to move out already. Still, there was one thing I could say.

They love each other.

They might be snooty, smug snobs most of the time,

but they do it together. They've got each other's backs. Their love is stable and, although I'd never admit it, is something I admire in them.

And now, that shatters. I don't have to question the validity of Mom's statement because I perhaps already knew. I knew that something didn't sit right. I knew by the way Dad's face burned with embarrassment when he saw me walk in that things were amiss.

But hearing the confirmation doesn't make it any easier. "Mom, I'm sorry," I say.

"No, I am," she whispers. "I shouldn't have said anything. This wasn't for you to know."

"Of course you should've told me. I'm sorry. Really, I am."

I get up from my seat and cross the floor, wrapping my mom in my arms. It's an uncharacteristically affectionate moment for us. We've never been the hugging, kissing type of family. In many ways, I've always been the outlier, the one on the outskirts not understanding what drives my parents. But now, nothing but sympathy rises up.

"So what now?" I whisper after a long moment when her tears have stopped. Mom shrugs.

"What do you mean?"

I study her. "I mean who is moving out? Did you file for divorce?"

She blinks at me before reaching for her wine glass.

"Mom?"

"Dear, it's not that simple, you know. There's business to think about, your legacy. Our image."

I feel anger writhing inside of me, replacing the sympathy. "Do not tell me you're taking him back."

"Darling, there's nothing that needs to change. This isn't something new. Sheila's been around for a while. It's just something I've learned to deal with. I'm just... I'm sad you had to find out is all."

"Wait, back up," I demand. "You've known about this?"

She wipes at her tears. "Darling, marriage isn't easy, okay? I know you can't understand at your age, but you will. And sometimes for the life we want, we make sacrifices. Concessions."

I shake my head. "I hate you," I whisper.

"Sage," she replies softly, but it's no use.

I'm gone in every way that matters.

Tears fall now, but this time they're from my eyes. I hate that I'm crying, hate that I expected so much more from two people who are clearly so emotionally clueless.

"How could you do this? Don't you have any pride?" I ask, shaking my head through the tears.

"Dear, it isn't about pride. Like I said, it's about image. It's about this life we have. Sure, there are some negatives, but overall, the positives make it worth sticking around."

I think about all the things I want to say, but instead, I spin on my heel, stomp up the stairs, and slam the door. She doesn't come after me. She never does.

I bury my head in the pillow, shattered and pissed that I've let them crush me. I shouldn't be surprised. So many things about my parents, this house, this family, are a façade. I guess just knowing the depth of the façade is a bit depressing.

Everything is a lie. They are a lie. The kisses, the midnight strolls on the beach, the summers in Manhattan exploring the city—it's all a lie. Dad's having an affair, and Mom's letting him. How sick is that? I might not know a lot about love, and I might be young, but I know that isn't what love looks like. And for what? Her image? Her money? The family legacy? What legacy is that?

I cry myself to sleep that night, mourning over a family, a truth that was never mine to have. And when I wake up, I shake it off like I have so many other things. I look myself in the eye in the mirror, studying my frizzy locks and smeared makeup.

I make two promises.

1. *I, Sage Everling, will not depend on my family for my success. I will do it myself. I will find pride in who I am and pride in chasing my passions while standing on my own two feet.*
2. *I will not let love take hold of me like it did my*

mother. I will not let my pride be shattered by a man. I will own my passions but not let them own me.

From that day on, the end of my relationship with my parents began, the fast unraveling of a thread that was always fraying. And, from that day on, Sage Everling, the woman who relied solely on herself, began her trek into the foreboding world, determined to make her mark in her own high heels and never settle for a life lived for someone else.

THAT FOURTEEN-YEAR-OLD GIRL WOULD BE PROUD, I think as I stare at the cover of a popular magazine. My photograph is on it, a sultry, serious pose I've become known for. The headline reads "Ocean City's Bachelorette Strikes Again With New Line." I should be thrilled to have a headline in a magazine, to have snagged this opportunity. I think my fourteen-year-old self would be proud of the confident, independent woman on this cover who did it all on her own.

Still, sitting here staring at the cover, thinking of all that's transpired, I see something I haven't quite detected before.

Loneliness.

Since that revelation in my mother's kitchen that night, I've been terrified to lean on another. I've been terrified to give up my passions like my mother did. I've been terrified of becoming a dependent housewife willing to look the other way and destroy her pride for the man she married.

Looking at the cover, I know I haven't done that. I've succeeded in avoiding those fates. Still, I wonder what I've sacrificed to earn that accomplishment—and how will that sacrifice affect me going forward? Have I failed to strike a balance between the two sentiments and, thus, done the very thing I was afraid of doing—selling my life out and losing out on a sense of fulfillment?

Maybe the convictions we settle on at fourteen aren't necessarily the beliefs we should shape our entire adult life around. And maybe that's on me and not my parents, I realize, the thought shattering any sense of confidence I had that I'm living the right way.

TWENTY-THREE

Sage

———

"THERE WILL BE TIME FOR CELEBRATING AFTER THIS launch," I argue into the phone, balancing it precariously between my ear and shoulder as I try to type up some emails.

"Sage, everything is ready to go. We've all done our part, and this launch is going to be fabulous. Now come on, let's go celebrate," Harper argues into the phone.

"I just want to do a few more things. We have a lot invested in this, and I want to make sure it's a success."

"It will be, but you're not going to be able to enjoy it because you're going to be burned out."

I sigh. Harper's probably, as usual, right.

For the past four days, I've been a whirlwind of business activity, essentially locking myself away in my condo to send more emails, reach out to more magazines, and just pour myself into this line. I tell myself it's because I want to make sure the line is successful, but if I'm being honest, there might be more at play.

"So what about Cash? Have you made any exceptions to your work-only rule for him?"

"No, he knows I'm busy."

Cash stopped by yesterday with coffee and wanting to play, but I politely declined. I could see the worry in his eye that I was regressing, but I reassured him I just needed time. Time and distance while I get this all sorted out.

"You're crazy."

"He knows work comes first."

"But maybe it shouldn't," Harper argues.

"Harper," I warn, shaking my head at the conversation we've had dozens of times.

"Okay, okay, I'm done. Now listen, I'll let you stay in your workaholic hole for the next few days, but once this line comes out, that's it. You're getting out and celebrating. I might make you take a whole month off. So enjoy your crazy little ways now."

Before I can argue, she hangs up, and I put the phone down, staring at the half-written email on my screen.

What am I doing?

I exhale, the question I've always known how to answer now seeming like an enigma. I look around my condo, which is stuffed full of fashion items and fabrics and files. I've built this online empire. I've created this brand, this success—but what's it all for? If, at the end of it all, I only have these emails, these files, and a silent condo, was it all worth it? The money, the public accolades—it's all great, but isn't there something more to all of this? Instantly, my mind goes to the one person who has stirred things up, who has made me wonder if, in fact, this life I've chosen is actually the right life for me.

Cash Creed.

I've spent my life priding myself on the fact that I don't need anyone to lean on, that no one gets my full commitment. But what if I've had it all wrong? Would leaning on someone be so bad? Would leaning on Cash Creed, building a life with him, really take away from all of this? And even if it did, would that be such a bad thing?

I stand and trudge over to my window, staring out at the tourist town below. I think about all that's happened to get me to this point, all of the decisions I've made. I think about that fourteen-year-old girl staring into the mirror and vowing to be nothing like her parents. But in this posh condo, all alone, with only money and business driving me, maybe I haven't succeeded at that very goal. Maybe I've, in a round-about way, turned into a version of them.

And that terrifies me.

Then again, is Cash Creed really the one who can change it all? Is he the one to put trust in? I've seen what happens when trust is violated in a relationship. When the player decides to play for keeps, is she really all that wise to choose another player, a man who is a self-proclaimed commitment-phobe?

My head swirls with questions and confusions. How did things get so messy? How did I get to this point?

Monticello rubs my leg, startling me out of my self-deprecating stupor. I take a deep breath, glance around the apartment, and decide it's time.

It's time to try something new. If it doesn't work out, well, I guess I'll just have to pick myself back up. After all, I've learned how to stand on my own two feet. What's the worst that can happen?

TWENTY-FOUR

Cash

After a long day at the apartment office dealing with all sorts of renter debacles, it feels good to sink into the sofa. Dammit, I must be getting old or losing my touch because usually on a Friday night, I'd be going out. Yet, here I am thinking about nothing but drinking beer and falling asleep. Shit, I've lost my touch. I've lost my sense of game.

Of course, I know it isn't just about energy levels. It's about a sexy, infuriatingly smart woman who won't let go of her grasp on me.

It's been a week since I've seen her, but she still lays claim to all of my thoughts. God, it's like I'm under some freaky spell of hers, one that makes me simultaneously yearn for her and fear her and her witchcraft-like ways. I feel like a lovesick teenager, and it's not a feeling familiar to me.

I've tried calling her, tried to make plans to see her, but she's busy with her upcoming line. While I find her workaholic drive sexy, I also find it worrisome. Maybe she's having second thoughts. Maybe this whole "let's get to know each other" vibe was just a trick, another one of her love traps. Falling in love with a player isn't advisable because you just never know when her heart can be trusted.

Still, I have to admit there's a rush there too, of knowing she's not easy to tame but trying my hardest anyway. I've never been one to shy away from a challenge, so why let this get the best of me?

I flip on the television as Killer jumps on my lap, ready to tuck in for the night. I'm starting to let my explicit thoughts of Sage take me off to dreamland, when there's a knock at the door. Killer emits a growl, and I sigh as I stand up, wondering who the hell it could be. When I fling open the door, though, confusion and excitement set in.

"Can I come in?" Sage says, her sultry voice reigniting the life in me.

"Sure," I murmur, rubbing a hand over my two-day stubble, wishing I'd have known she was coming over. She's in jeans and a simple T-shirt, but she still looks phenomenal as she struts into the kitchen, a six-pack of beer in her hand.

"So, I know flowers are typically the protocol, at least from what I've seen in movies, but I thought you'd appreciate this more," she says, handing the beer over to me. I set it on the counter and raise an eyebrow.

"Protocol for what?"

"A date," she says, her bright lips curving into a nervous smile. "I know, I know, dates are against your rules. Mine too. But, you know, with this whole getting to know you thing, we've kept it so informal and all of that. We haven't used labels or whatever. So Cash Creed, I want to shake it up. I want to officially take you on an honest date, you know food, small talk, the whole thing."

I stare at her, shaking my head.

"Is that a no?" she asks, concern creeping in.

I cross the floor, closing the gap between us, and take her into my arms. I plant a kiss hard and fast on those bright red lips, silencing any doubt. It feels good to have her in my arms again, to be close, to feel her. I've been starving for her, in truth.

"I've missed you," I reply simply.

"I've missed you, too," she says. "Which is why I thought it was time for a date. No bars or hot sex or any of the stuff we're used to. Just you and me, some food, and some real date-like behaviors."

"I'm in. Let me change," I say, looking at my scuffed-up jeans and T-shirt.

"No, don't. Let's keep it simple," she replies, and I can't resist agreeing. This woman's got me hooked so bad, I'd do anything. Almost anything she wanted.

"So where to?" I ask.

"I have a plan," she says, leaving it at that.

"Whoa, hold up. I don't like surprises," I respond honestly.

"Is that because you have power issues?" she asks coyly as I follow her out into the sticky night air.

"No, it's because I like to be prepared."

"Well, Cash Creed, tonight, I've got the reins. I'm taking the lead. Can you be okay with that?"

And for once, I think I can.

***

THE SUN IS SETTING WHEN WE GET TO THE SAND, BOTH of us loaded up like pack mules with chairs, the picnic basket, and the blanket. We get organized, plopping the blanket down as I weight it with the chairs, the night breeze from the ocean threatening to lift it away.

"Nice night," I say, honestly, as Sage sits down and

begins to unpack the basket. It's filled with takeout from different local haunts—seafood, cheeses, crackers, cheesecake from the little bakery down the street.

She grins at me, shrugging. "I'm not a fantastic cook," she admits. "But it's the thought that counts, right?"

"To the thought," I say, holding up a bottle of water to toast her.

"So what's new in the world of Cash Creed?" she asks after we've both taken a sip.

Nothing. Thinking of you. Pining for a woman against my better judgement. These are the things I should say. But I don't. I simply shrug, setting down my drink.

"Work. That's about it. You?"

"Same. Jesus, we're turning into rather boring people, huh?"

"Speak for yourself," I tease.

"Well, I am. I've spent the week locked away working like crazy."

"I mean, I assume running Evermore does take a lot of time," I offer, and she glances at me.

"It does. Not that I'm complaining. I'm proud of what I've built. But doing it all from the ground up alone wasn't a walk in the park. I guess that's why I work so hard now. I know what it took to build it. I don't want to slip off, to let it crumble."

I study the sexy entrepreneur sitting on the blanket beside me, and I see something I didn't see that first night. Vulnerability. Talking about her fear of failure, I see a softer side to the confident woman she projects. And I recognize it. Because I think deep down, in every confident woman or man, there's a bit of a fearful side, too.

"Tell me about it. About how you got started," I say, leaning back on my elbows now as I stare at the waves crashing.

"I'm sure you don't want to hear all about my fashion company."

"What's that supposed to mean? I've clearly got mad style. What, you think I'm not into fashion?"

She raises an eyebrow. "Not my kind of fashion."

"Well, I still want to hear about it. Come on. Isn't that what tonight's about?"

She takes another sip of her drink. "Well, I grew up in a bit of a lavish lifestyle. Not that I'm bragging because well, I hated it. I had basically everything I could've wanted, material wise. We went on extravagant vacations, and I saw more of the world by the age of eight than most people our age. Still, I never liked what we had as a family."

She takes another sip of her drink, pausing before continuing. I sense this isn't easy for her to talk about.

Regardless, I don't interrupt her, letting her get her bearings before continuing on.

"My parents always expected me to just carry on the family legacy, the family business, but I knew by my teens I wanted nothing of the sort. I didn't want to be my mother, depending on a man who clearly wasn't trustworthy. I felt like my family was just a lie, a fraud. I wanted to get away and do something on my own without them. I wanted to show them that I wasn't them."

"Why was that so important?" I ask, hesitating after the words are out. Maybe I'm prodding too much.

She turns and looks at me, those eyes I've come to appreciate showing a lot of pain. "I've never talked about this."

"You can trust me," I whisper, covering her hand with my own, our skin electric at the touch. She inhales, and I can tell she's holding back tears.

"My dad had an affair on my mother. For most of my life."

"I'm sorry," I say, seeing Sage, the hurt woman instead of Sage the powerful businesswoman before me.

"Well, she wasn't. My mom knew about it. All of it. She stood by, playing at the façade because she was too afraid to lose the life she had. She depended on my father for everything, and she was so addicted to their lifestyle she was willing to push her pride down for him. When I found out about it, I vowed that would never be me. I wouldn't let a man or anyone do that to me. I would build myself, my life, on my own. I would find the confidence and pride she didn't have. That's why I started Evermore. It's about me building my life, but it's also about giving other people confidence in theirs. My pieces are bold, and I want them to be. I want people to be unapologetic in their fashion and in their lives. It was part of my mission."

"That's... wow," I reply, feeling like an idiot but not knowing what to say. So much of her makes sense now.

"I'm sorry," she says. "I didn't mean to dump on you."

"It's okay. I'm glad you did. It makes sense now."

"What?" she asks.

"Everything. You. Your rules about love." I reach up and tuck a wayward strand of her hair behind her ear, studying her face. She swipes at her eyes, trying to brush away the tears ready to fall. I grab her hand and pull it away.

"It's okay to be vulnerable. It's okay to admit you've been hurt, Sage. That doesn't take away any of your strength."

She studies me for a long minute. "Says the man who has just as much of a wall up as I do."

The words cut into me, coming from her beautiful lips as her eyes pierce into mine.

She's right. She's so right. Sage's walls, her rules, her attack on love makes so much sense now. It comes from a place of protection, thanks to a past that has haunted her. It comes from a place of devotion to her mantra.

Where the hell does mine come from? I have nothing like Sage's past to blame. I came from a loving family that was nothing but supportive. Mom and Dad might not be perfect, but they certainly raised me with more love than material things. They are the epitome of unconditional love, not just for their kids but for each other. They've been the best example of what love could be. So what's my excuse? Why do I put up these walls? For so long, I've said it's all about fun. But is it? And, more importantly, can those walls ever come down?

"You're right. You're so right. I don't have a good reason for it, either. I'm just fucked-up when it comes to love, I guess. Maybe I'm just an asshole. I don't know."

Now it's her turn to comfort me. She puts a soft,

delicate hand on my jaw, raising my head to look at her. Her eyes are smoldering, fiery, and unapologetic.

"You're not an asshole or fucked-up. You're just you, Cash. And well, maybe you just haven't found the person to change your mind about love. Maybe she just hasn't come along just yet."

I stare, and I feel the walls slowly start to crumble. I start to see a different kind of fun right here with the woman on the blanket beside me. I see that sometimes loving and leaving isn't what's best. Sometimes loving and staying has its benefits, too.

"Or maybe I have," I whisper, leaning in to close the gap between us. I quiet the vulnerabilities vibrating in both of our chests tonight. I shut down all the psychological fears and all of the past hurts and all of the past mistakes.

I kiss Sage Everling like I've never kissed another, and maybe in some ways, I haven't. I don't know if it's the magical feeling of the cloudless sky above us, the sound of the waves, or the fact that we've just worn each other down. I don't know if it's the way she says my name or the fact that she's opened up to me tonight with a genuineness I've never experienced with anyone else. I don't know if it's because for the first time, I feel like someone has seen right through me, right to my core, and didn't go running.

Good or bad, I know that with this kiss tonight, we've turned a corner. Two players discovering that playing for keeps might be a possibility after all. It's scary as hell, but it's also something else, I realize as we pull back from the kiss, both staring at each other with an intensity bubbling from within.

It's also affirmation that maybe we're both not as broken as we once thought.

Sage

I DESPERATELY WANT CASH CREED TO TAKE ME HOME after our picnic confessions on the beach. I want him to toss me on my bed and continue the kiss from where it left off. I want him to make me forget about the past and the complications of love by screwing my brains out, by spending the night in the throes of passion. But, to my surprise, he stands outside my condo door after we've packed up and decides to call it a night.

"I had a great time with you," he says after pulling back from a sweet, simple kiss.

"Call me?" I ask, grinning.

"You better believe it," he replies, and I chuckle.

"Is that the first time you've ever said that and meant it?" I ask.

He pretends to take mental inventory before responding. "I reckon it is."

"Careful, your Texas is showing."

"Because I said reckon?"

I just nod, grinning.

"Keep it up, and I'll show you that what they say is true. You know, about everything being bigger in Texas." He pulls me in, teasing me with another kiss, with his tongue.

"Been there, done that, remember?" His kiss ignites me, though, and I feel the need to pull him into my condo, to explore him all over again.

"You're right. You already know how impressive I am. So I guess we can call it a night."

"You can come in," I quickly reply, hating the desperation in my voice, the hungry need that can be heard in my tone. I bite my lip.

His eyes sparkle, and I think he's going to take me up on it. I think that finally this sexual tension between us can be put to rest.

He leans in, kisses me again, teasing me. "Good-night, Sage," he says, just when I'm about to go crazy.

"Are you serious?" I ask, leaning against my door.

"Come on. I have to keep you somewhat intrigued now that we've turned a corner."

"I'm already intrigued," I argue.

"I know. Let's keep it that way."

"Fine. I didn't want to have sex with you anyway," I reply, crossing my arms and raising an eyebrow.

"Sure you didn't. But I'm just following your rules. You know, about no sex, just a date. You'll thank me."

I shake my head, exasperated. "Goodnight, Cash."

He winks before strolling away, turning back to give me a lusty final glance.

I let myself into my condo, groaning. Still, as I climb into bed alone, I smile thinking about our night on the beach. It was a night like I haven't had forever—a real date, real conversation, and no sexuality driving every move.

Even though I fall asleep unsatisfied in so many ways, I grin to myself thinking about how intrigued I am—and how maybe Cash Creed could be the one to finally break all of my rules.

TWENTY-SIX

Sage

———

"THIS ISN'T REALLY A CHAMPAGNE KIND OF MORNING," I murmur, swiping at the mascara streaks on my face. I don't even know what I'm wearing to be honest, but I know I look like a wreck. Harper saunters through my door carrying two bottles of champagne and still wearing a smile.

"Chin up, lovely. This is exactly the kind of morning for champagne."

She walks to the cabinet that houses my glasses and pulls two out. I slump over on the island. This was supposed to be a champagne popping kind of morning, smiles and pride for what we'd accomplished with the new Evermore line. Instead, it's been a tears in my coffee, sweatpants kind of morning.

The launch of Evermore's Everpure line, a lofty,

minimalist line for both men and women, was supposed to be the launch of my career. It was going to take us to even bigger heights, get us on every single celebrity's must-have list. We were going to soar.

Instead, this morning's reviews are touting the line as "overrated", "unimaginative", and even "abysmal", citing the launch as "lazy" and "lacking vision". Just like that, the success we've achieved from building this company has been overshadowed by this one thing we've worked so hard on.

"Hey, so a few reviewers don't like it. So what."

"They're not just any reviewers," I murmur as she slides me some champagne. She pours herself a glass of orange juice and joins me at the island.

She's smiling that typical Harper smile, but I can tell she's burning inside, too. These were largely her designs, not that I'm blaming her. We're in this together. But I know it has to sting to see some of the commentaries on her designs.

"Look, the big magazines and influencers just don't get it. That doesn't mean it's going to be a total failure. Your fans are still going to love the items, and we'll just have to maybe change up our marketing. It's going to be okay."

I look at my best friend, the reassurance in her eyes. Still, I can't see the truth in her words. Instead, I see the word "failure" written in the stars. I see the failure my parents always warned me would come.

I hate that today they've been proven right. I bet wherever they are, if they've come out of their selfish bubbles for five minutes to take in the world around them, they're smiling at the disappointment of Evermore's newest line.

"I just thought this was going to be a win. We put so much into this one," I whine, hating the tone of my voice. I'm unable to stop it.

"I know. But listen, some lines start out like this. I mean, other fashion houses have had lines that got terrible reviews and turned out just fine. And this isn't our only launch. We have the Evervibe line we've started planning, you know? It's going to be okay."

"I know. It just sucks."

"It does. I agree with you there. So that's why I brought two bottles. Drink your face off today, watch some movies, relax. Take some time to just recover, and then we'll be right back at it. And those critics will be sorry they ever said those things about you. Because the next launch is going to be epic."

I wish I had her optimism. Because right now, all I can wonder is if Evermore has seen its best days.

Harper leans on my shoulder. "It'll be okay, boss lady. I love you. I'm proud of you."

"Ditto. I think your designs are great," I say as she sits back up. I chug down a glass of champagne, slamming it a bit too hard on the island when it's gone. "If those hoity-toity critics can't see that, then you know what I say? I say fuck them."

"That's the spirit. That's the Sage Everling we know and love. Now listen, you know I draw best when I'm angry and mopey. And today, I'm sort of both. So I'm going to go work on the Evervibe sketches. Do you need anything before I go?"

"I have all I need," I reply, feigning a smile as I point to the champagne.

"Call me if you need anything."

"You do the same." I lean in and hug her before walking her to the door.

"Are you sure you're okay?" she asks, turning one more time to study me.

I offer my best "I'm fine" look, nod, and give her a thumbs up.

"Okay," she says hesitantly before heading out. I slowly shut the door after waving one more time.

And then I crumple to the floor and cry. No matter how sassy and confident, every woman has her breaking point. Every woman can only fake being okay for so long.

And every woman has her ultimate fear that cracks her.

"Shit," I murmur, looking down at my sweatpants that are now covered in cheese puff crumbs and my champagne-stained T-shirt. I run a hand through my frizzy bun, knowing it's no use. I wipe underneath my eyes, knowing my mascara's just smeared even more, and pause the chick flick I've been watching.

"Coming," I yell before traipsing to the door. I figure it's probably Harper coming back to check on me or to show me some designs she's excited about. I whip open the door, Barcelona and Monticello meowing at my feet. They always rush to greet company.

And then the second "Shit" slips out as I see who's at the door.

The first thing I notice is the bouquet of red roses he's extending to me. The second thing I notice? He's wearing an Everpure outfit, head to toe. And although right now, it's sort of a slap in the face, I also notice it looks absolutely gorgeous on him. I doubt anyone could give this outfit a bad review if they saw it on Cash Creed, the way it hugs the lines of his chiseled body. Killer ambles through the door, taking ownership of the place, and the cats hiss, but I don't take my eyes off of Cash.

"Hey," he says, as I gawk, remembering suddenly what I must look like. He's never seen me like this. Hell, I don't know that any man has.

"Sorry, I'm…. Well, I wasn't expecting anyone."

"I wanted to surprise you. Can I come in?" he asks, gesturing inside. The cats are still meowing, and I actually have to shove Monticello with my foot so he doesn't wander out.

"Yeah, come in," I say because what else can I say when he's standing in my doorway holding flowers and my cats are ready to escape?

He hands me the roses, and this time I take them, still feeling flustered. "Thanks. What are these for?"

"I know your launch of Everpure just happened. I wanted to congratulate you. Hence the outfit. I think I was the first purchase when the website went live. Stunning, right? If you need a new male model, you know I could kill it, right?" His smile is huge as he does a model-like walk and spin. I just stare at him, grinning in spite of the situation.

"Thank you. I think. But I'm guessing you didn't read the fashion critiques or reviews this morning."

"What?" he asks, looking at me like I've spoken a foreign language. "There are fashion critics?"

"Yeah," I murmur, wandering to the cupboard to find my vase. It takes a while to find one, and I have to blow some dust off of it. I put the bouquet of roses in and admire it. I can't remember the last time a man bought me flowers.

"Well, I don't need to read reviews. I have my own sense of fashion. If you couldn't tell, I'm sort of serious about the way I look, and I have to say, I didn't think anything could make this ass look better than it already does. I stand corrected because these pants hug me in all the right ways. Don't you think?"

I roll my eyes, shaking my head.

"I have to admit," he begins, walking closer to me. "I don't know a lot about fashion designing and what you do. But I don't know, I imagined you'd be like wearing an outfit from the line yourself, having a lavish party or something today. Not that I think what you're doing is bad. I like the laid-back vibe you like never give off. You look sexy in a vulnerable way."

"I look like shit," I say, rolling my eyes at him. He continues walking toward me.

"Truth bomb. You could never look like shit."

"Truth bomb?" I ask, grinning. "Who says that?"

"This stud man," he says, pointing to himself.

I roll my eyes again, but I have to admit he's lightened the mood. "What is wrong with you?"

"For starters, I've missed you. I know you've been busy and all, but Jesus, girl, you need to get out of this place. Have some fun. Isn't that the perk of owning your own business?"

"Yeah, well, not really feeling like showing my face right now."

"What are you talking about?"

I sigh as he puts his hands on my waist. I look up into those eyes that do make me feel vulnerable. I tell myself not to cry as I proceed to tell him what the reviewers and critics have said.

"So what?" he asks, shrugging.

I look at him, stupefied. "So what? Are you kidding? These reviewers and critics can make or break you. They've basically sealed the fate of this line. I've poured so much into this line, and it's done before it even had a chance." Tears start to well no matter how hard I fight them. When they spill over, Cash reaches up and gently wipes them away, his strong hands feeling powerful against my fragile state.

"Listen to me," he practically whispers, so close we could kiss but don't. "Don't let them tear down your work, your vision. In all seriousness, Sage, you're amazing. Look at what you've accomplished, what you've built."

"Yeah, and now I've failed."

He shakes his head. "No way. Not possible. So some stuck-up fashion critics don't get your vision. Who cares? Other people will. And you haven't failed. Look at what you've done already. You're this force in the business world, an indie business that has risen to the top. You're on the same level with some of those upper crust fashion houses—and you did it yourself, all the way. That's amazing. You're this sexy, gorgeous woman with a heart of gold. You're daring and bold, but you're also rational and witty. You're this perfect concoction of everything a person could want to be, and you've achieved your dreams. That's beautiful. That's successful. I don't give a shit what some fashion 'expert' says about it."

I study the man saying these things about me, and it's like I'm seeing him for the first time, hearing these things for the first time. So many men have whispered sweet nothings to me, all with a motive behind them. These words, though, come from Cash's lips with a pure quality that could make me cry a whole new set of tears.

It's like he sees me for who I am, even standing here in these ratty sweatpants and frizzy hair. It's not about who I pretend to be with Cash. It's not about the sexy, sex-loving Sage when I'm with him. It's about just Sage, the woman I want to be, flaws and failures and everything else.

He isn't standing here with me to celebrate my success. He's standing here to hold me when I feel like a failure. He's standing here telling me I'm beautiful when I feel far from it. He's here to share in all of me, to share all of him with me, and to just be the two people we are. For the first time in a long time, I feel like I can be the real Sage, the one who is confident and powerful—but also scared and vulnerable and not quite all put together sometimes.

And that is probably the sexiest thing I've ever felt. That's probably the best gift he could've given me: a gift no roses or expensive clothes could outshine. I put my arms around his neck and pull him in closer, taking his lips in mine, owning him with a passion I let fly off the handle.

As my hands wander down the buttons on his shirt, I whisper, "This shirt looks super sexy on you. And I know for a fact you paid a lot for it. But I'm going to have to get rid of it right now, if you're okay with that." I pull his shirt apart, popping all the buttons open in a rough but suave move. I peel it off of him, admiring his body as I toss the shirt across the kitchen. He picks me up and puts me on the counter.

"I don't mind one bit, Miss Everling. In fact, if I had known the shirt would have inspired such fantasies, I'd have asked for the prototype months ago."

His hands find the hem of my T-shirt, and he helps me lift it over my head. I pull the ponytail holder out of my bun, letting my frizzy hair fall to my shoulders. As we claw and paw at each other, the hunger of a passion unsatisfied since that first time we slept together, I let my mind go numb to the outside world. I put aside the line and Evermore and think about only one thing—the roaring fire I feel when I'm with Cash Creed, and how for once, I'm more than okay with experiencing that.

We spend the afternoon breaking all of our "one and done" sort of rules as we hit three and four and eventually five. Later, curled up in my bed debating over whether we should call for Chinese takeout or pizza, Cash turns to me.

"Today was amazing," he murmurs, kissing my forehead.

And, despite all the things that went oh-so-wrong with today, despite all of the issues with my company and all of the reasons I should be devastated, I couldn't agree with Cash more.

"Thank you," I reply, kissing his jawline.

"For what?" he grins, and I playfully hit him.

"For everything," I say, falling into his eyes again as I fall victim to his hands once more.

"WHAT ARE YOU DOING?" CASH ASKS, WIPING THE SLEEP from his eyes as he stumbles into my kitchen. I'm wearing his shirt—and his shirt only—and sitting at the kitchen island, working on plans.

"I'm inspired. I'm drawing up plans and marketing ideas for the next launch."

"What the hell time is it?" he groggily asks as he stumbles toward me in his boxers, planting a kiss on my neck.

"Five."

"Jesus. Do you always get up this early?"

I shrug. "Got to get going in the morning if you want to be successful."

He makes what sounds like a groan as he stumbles over to my Keurig. "I take it you're not a morning person?" I ask as I motion toward the cupboard with coffee mugs.

"That's a no."

"Well, just give me like ten minutes here, and then I'll whip up some breakfast."

He pauses at the coffee maker, eyeing me. "You know, I can think of much better things we can do for ten minutes." He winks at me, and I shake my head.

"Only ten minutes? Please, darling. You're going to have to entice me with better promises than that."

He shakes his head as the hot liquid spews out. He wanders over to the island, taking a peek at what I'm working on.

"It's good to see you inspired, to see you not letting yesterday get to you," he says seriously, warming his hands on the mug.

I look up at him. "I have you to thank. You helped me get out of my funk."

"Yeah, well, I guess like six times will do that for you."

"I think it was five. But who's counting?"

"It was definitely six. And I'm counting. When you're that impressive, you have to keep tally." He winks at me, and I shake my head.

"Wonder why you've never been serious about anyone," I retort.

"Who says I haven't been?"

"You told me yourself," I reply as he wanders around the island, kissing my neck again.

"Yeah, well, people change," he whispers into my hair before spinning me around on my stool and kissing me hard.

As his lips wander to the right spot on my neck, I bite my lip.

Yes, they do, I think as he leads me to the shower to get clean after we get dirty yet again.

Cash

"I MUST ADMIT THAT SHOWER MIGHT BE THE BEST ONE I've ever done it in," I say, running a hand through my wet hair as Sage kisses my cheek. I kiss her neck again, and she giggles.

"Stop, I have to get some work done."

"Says who?" I ask as we head to the kitchen to get some more coffee.

I'm getting ready to debate with her the benefits of another day romping in the sheets when there's a knock at the door. Before we can head to get it, the door flies open and in walks a girl with black braids, overalls, and a neon orange shirt on.

A girl that looks very familiar.

"Oh, wow. Sorry, Sage! Hi. Hi, Cash. I was just coming over to show you some of my work from yesterday, but I didn't mean to interrupt." She talks a mile a minute, taking over the room like the sight of her neon clothing. She beams at the sight of us, and I notice Sage blushing.

"Looks like you got through the day yesterday just fine, though," the girl murmurs.

"Um, Cash, this is Harper, my best friend and business associate."

I look at the girl who grins, and recognition sinks in. "I know you, don't I?" I ask.

Harper shrugs coyly. "Small town, so maybe."

"It's hardly a small town. You were the one from the dog park."

As if on cue, Killer dashes over and starts barking at Harper's feet. She picks up the dog, who instantly calms at her touch.

"Like I said, small town. Anyway, I don't want to interrupt. I should be going," Harper says, putting Killer down and picking up Monticello instead. The cats have already grown accustomed to Killer, apparently.

"No, it's okay. I should get going. I have to take care of some things in the office anyway."

"You sure?" Sage asks, eyeing me.

"Wouldn't want to stop you from working today, and I feel like if I stay you might be tempted to shove all thoughts of work aside." I sidle up to her, wrapping an arm around her waist. I feel her body lean into me, and I have to remind myself that we have an audience.

"That's what I'm talking about. Damn girl, you went all in," Harper replies, and Sage laughs.

"Call me later?" Sage asks as I kiss her cheek.

"Forward much?" I tease.

"Always," she replies back.

"God, if you two weren't so damn beautiful together, I might gag a little. But anyway, lover boy, good seeing you again. Hope to see you around more often," Harper says, giving me a playful shove as I gather Killer and head out the door.

On my way to the rental office, I can't stop grinning like a damn fool. I replay our moments over and over, thinking about what it was like to wake up to Sage, to fall into a comfortable, playful routine. My mind starts dancing over thoughts I've never considered—like what it would be like to wake up to her every morning.

Dangerous. Dangerous territory, Cash.

My heart freezes up at the realization. I need to slow down. Because if I'm not careful, I'm going to be all in. All the way in with no chips left in my pocket at all.

TWENTY-EIGHT

Sage

———

"Look at us, being all conventional," I murmur over a plate of pasta and the glass of wine in front of me. I've put on my favorite black dress, and Cash looks like pure lust in his suit and his tie a little undone. He's got that two-day stubble that makes me go crazy if a man pulls it off just right—and Cash pulls it off and then some.

"Hey, this was your idea. I was fine dining in," Cash replies with a smirk, his foot finding mine under the table.

"We have to eat sometime, and if we're not in public, I feel like you won't give me a moment to do anything but romp with you."

"Like you mind," he teases.

I take a sip of my wine in response.

Because the truth is—I don't mind. Not one bit.

For the past few days, Cash has been in my condo more than he hasn't been. It's like now that we've crossed the bridge, gotten over our insecurities, there's no stopping us. I've realized how amazing it is to have someone to share my life with, even the humdrum, daily life parts. Waking up in his arms, eating breakfast together. It's suddenly become worthwhile. It's like a new part of me is alive, one I didn't know had faded away.

I look at the man across the table and think about all the reservations we've fought through to get to this point. I think about how the Sage from a few months ago would have vomited to hear my cheesy sentiments, to see how utterly crazy I am for the dark-eyed Texan I'm now sharing Italian cuisine with.

I think about how easy it would be to take a step back, to return to that guarded-heart Sage who convinced herself she didn't care about anything but work and sex. But looking at Cash, I think about how I don't want to do anything of the sort.

The words spew out before I can stop them, but in truth, I'm glad. I don't want to stop them. The walls are down now, and I'm a forward person. I go after what I want with reckless abandon, without hesitation or pause.

And he's a cause worth chasing.

"I'm falling for you, Cash Creed," I whisper just a decibel over the cheesy music playing in the restaurant. His eyes stare into mine, perusing me with a languid tenacity.

"I've already fallen for you, Sage Everling."

Dinner continues with a newfound sense of intimacy, of trust, and of a promise that we're not going back to where we came from. We're in new territory— but we're traversing it together, always together. Nothing's changing that.

It's a risk, it's true. There are no promises in love, even if you're playing for keeps.

But we're both playing now, all in. Completely and utterly all in.

We go home to my place, and in the darkness of my room, I know that there's absolutely no going back. He possesses me now, in every way imaginable.

And for once, I'm fine that someone else is taking the reins.

TWENTY-NINE

Sage

———

"Here they come," a voice announces from the bar as I walk into the Marooned Pirate on Cash's arm. It's odd walking into the place without having to hunt for a man.

"Is it weird not coming alone?" Cash asks, turning to me, as if he's read my mind.

I grin. "Who says I'm not?" I tease.

He pokes me playfully in the ribs, and I let out a squeal.

"Drinks on me," Reed assures as we take our place near the rest of Cash's friends. "We have lots to celebrate."

"Like?" the blonde-haired girl asks. Cash tells me her name is Avery.

"Like, our Texan has finally snagged the girl of his dreams," Reed says, holding up his margarita in a mock cheer.

"More like you snagged the bag of your dreams," Lysander replies, and I grin.

"Well, that too. But still, seriously, you two look amazing together," Reed responds.

Cash gets me a drink at the bar, and we head to the corner table. I settle in with Cash's friends, feeling like one of the group. It's surprisingly nice to be here, no pressure to find a man, no pretenses. Just me, a drink, and the man I'm crazy about beside me.

"So, brother, no conquests tonight?" Levi teases, nudging Cash.

"Oh, I have a conquest. She's just a guaranteed one," Cash replies.

"Don't be so sure," I sassily retort, downing my drink and dragging him to the dance floor. A fast song comes on, one of my favorites, and we shimmy to the middle, dancing like no one's watching.

I know, in fact, that everyone is watching. I've seen the whispers.

"You know, we might end up on the front page again," I murmur to Cash.

He grins and winks. "I'm counting on it." He takes

my jaw in his hands and kisses me wildly, recklessly. When he pulls away, I'm breathless.

"That was…."

"Amazing?" He teases. "Hey, I've got to give the press something good to gawk at if they're going to plaster us on the paper."

Eventually the rest of the crew joins us, and we dance and laugh. At some point, we all head back to Midsummer Nights for another round of drinks and a round of Reed's signature drunken french fries… really just french fries with every ingredient imaginable shoved on top. Sitting at the table getting to know the people Cash calls friends and family, I have a vision of us doing something like this every week. I think about the camaraderie, the connections I've been craving and didn't realize it.

This is family, I realize. This is life. Being together with people who don't care about your money or successes or what you're wearing. Smiling and laughing and just living. This is what I want forever.

Forever.

It's a word that still sends a chill through me. But when Cash and I say goodbye to the group of friends and head back to his place to mix it up—and to let Killer out—I think about what the word means and how maybe someday, just maybe it wouldn't be so scary. Not if Cash was the one crawling into bed with me, not if he was the one I was saying forever to.

It's crazy how a summer can change everything.

And it's crazy how sometimes it doesn't.

THIRTY

Cash

____

"ARE YOU SURE IT'S OKAY? ARE YOU SURE YOU DON'T need me to come home?" I ask again, afraid that Mama is lying. I listen carefully to every lilt in her voice, trying to discern whether or not she's telling the truth. I've gotten pretty good at detecting lies, thanks to the whole lawyer job and all.

"I'm sure, Cash. He's just taking some time off. Doctor's orders. He just needs to relax a little bit. We're fine. We have the two new interns. It'll be good to give them experience."

When I called to check in at home and find out how the firm is doing without me, I didn't expect this. I didn't expect to hear that Dad had a health scare and that he's taking time off from the firm. I panicked, instantly. How would they keep it going? Maybe I needed to get home.

But Mama reassured me it was fine, and that they would hold down the fort until I got back. I sighed in relief.

It was a conundrum, in reality. I missed the firm, the hustle and bustle and the confidence I had in my work. I was a way better lawyer than a landlord, and I wasn't afraid to admit it. Fixing broken pipes and dealing with late rent wasn't nearly as satisfying as being in the courtroom.

But there was one thing being a landlord touted that Texas and the family business couldn't—and I was enjoying every single waking second with her. Still, I had been crushing a rising fear in the past few days, and Dad's health scare wasn't helping.

What would happen at the end of summer? What would happen to us?

A part of me wished I could be like Levi, happy to start over in Ocean City, happy to stay. But that was him, not me. I have a career. I'm needed at home to help with the firm. I can't just abandon that for a sexy girl who may or may not be completely stealing all the parts of my heart.

Can I?

I shove the thought aside, heading into the shelter.

It's a rare morning I'm not with Sage. I had stepped out to get some work done at the office before our volunteer hours. As I drive the few miles to the shelter, though, I can't help but thinking about what we're going to do when summer ends—and how goodbye is going to feel

---

I PUT BOBO BACK IN HIS CAGE. THOSE BROWN EYES GET to me every time. It kills me to say no to him every Sunday. So many times, I thought about just trying him out, seeing if Killer could accept him. After all, attitudes change. Look at me and Sage.

I head over to the cat room, sitting beside Sage as she pets a new intake, Marlo. We talk and laugh about his antics when Janice pops her head in.

"You two look mighty cozy," Janice says, winking.

"Oh, no, we're not...." Sage begins, but then she stops herself. It's like an automatic reaction. She turns to me apologetically, but I squeeze her shoulder in reassurance. "Well, we are. It's complicated.... It's...."

"Isn't it always, honey?" Janice says, smirking and chuckling as she walks away.

"No, it's not complicated," Sage whispers, leaning

in to kiss my cheek before reaching out to pet Marlo. "Not anymore."

I watch her care for the cat, think about her words, and think about how crazy it is that Ocean City, that this girl, has changed my heart in such a short time.

We have a good rest of our day. When we leave, I make our usual stop. The tar-like coffee hasn't grown on us much, but I guess the tradition has. The Coffee Hole has a table waiting for us. In truth, no one else ever visits, so it's not really an achievement that we find a spot. We settle in and chat about our morning, about the new cats, and about the dog who got adopted. I brave a sip of the tepid beverage before I speak up.

"I'm going to miss working here. I mean, we have nice shelters back in Texas, but this one is just so sweet." I squeeze her hand across the table, thinking about how hard it's going to be when I have to fly back. Maybe I could take Bobo with me. Maybe Mama and Dad could use a new dog. I'm tossed out of my thoughts, though, by Sage's panicked words.

"What do you mean?" she asks, staring at me.

I set my coffee down. "I mean when I go back at the end of the summer. I've got my job, my place back home. I've already talked to Levi about bowing out sometime at the end of August. I feel bad leaving him with such a mess, but what can I do? I told him I wasn't cut out for the job." I wait for Sage to laugh about all that I've messed up at the apartments, but she doesn't.

She blinks. "So you're going back?"

Now I'm the one who is confused. I thought she knew this. "Well, yeah, Sage. This was always just a summer thing. I have to get back to my career, to my place back home."

"I see," she says, but clearly she doesn't. Tension becomes palpable.

"Sage, look, I know we've turned a corner. We started out the summer as two players playing a hand of love. And it's been amazing. It really has. But we never expected any of this. I can't just walk away from my career. This isn't home for me. I have to go back. My parents need me back at the firm." I think about Daddy, having a health scare and an anxiety attack. I think about Mama trying to juggle it all.

"And so that's it? What about us?"

"Well, I'm sure we can figure it out. We'll figure it out."

"I see." She glares at me for a long time.

I sigh. This is why we shouldn't have crossed that line. This is why we should have kept things free and fun. Because looking across the table at her, it almost kills me. It destroys me to see her breaking inside. It destroys me to think of saying goodbye. It kills me that this has gotten so complicated, and that even when two players commit to something real, it can't work out. Maybe we were fucking fools to think it would ever work out.

There's an icy silence between us before she finally stands.

"You know what, it doesn't matter. *This* doesn't matter."

And with the words out that can't be taken back, Sage stomps across the Coffee Hole, stomps on our progress we made, and slams the door on more than just a dilapidated coffee spot.

THIRTY-ONE

Sage

"ROOM SERVICE, HERE. I'VE GOT ALL THE ESSENTIALS." Her perky voice echoes through the entranceway to the condo. I hear Monticello and Barcelona's cacophony of cries rush towards the door to greet Harper. I don't move from my spot on the couch.

I hate that he's done this to me. Dammit. Dammit love and Cash Creed and my own stupidity. What the hell was I thinking? I've been burned before. I've always known love doesn't work. Why had I let myself get wrapped up in the damn fantasy? I was a fool. A fool who deserves to die lonely and miserable in this tiny apartment surrounded by cats, wearing crusty sweatpants and three-day-old hair.

Harper rushes into the living room. She startles at the sight. "Damn girl, I knew you needed some time alone. But have you moved from that sofa? My good-ness. I love you, and you always look amazing, but geez. I didn't realize the state of things had reached this point."

I look up at her. "I'm fine."

Harper raises an eyebrow. "Don't lie to me."

I sigh. "Look, I'm fine. I just... I'm pissed. Pissed that I let everyone convince me this whole love thing was going to work."

"Damn. Love. I haven't heard you throw that word around since... well, ever." Harper sits on the sofa by me, leaning in for a hug. "I brought you some wine and some ice cream. But I don't know. We might need something stronger."

Tears start to fall, and I hate myself for it.

"Hey, come on. It's going to be okay. Talk to me. Let's figure this out."

"There's nothing to figure out, Harper. I let my guard down like an idiot. I fell for him. And now he's leaving like none of it mattered."

"Well, you knew he wasn't staying forever, right? He has his job to think about. Imagine if roles were reversed."

I hate that this had made sense. I hate that I had opened my heart, and now the fairy tale is crashing down. Why couldn't it work out like the movies? Cash, giving up his life in Texas to be with me. Isn't that how it was supposed to work out? Doesn't love conquer all?

And is that what this is? Love? How dumb was I, how weak, throwing that word around?

I swipe at my tears. "I'm fine. I've cried it out of my system, cried him out of my system. We've got the new line to think about. I'm ready to get back to work." I stand from the couch, but Harper pulls my arm and yanks me back down.

"Stop it. Stop it right now. I know you can't just shove him aside that easily. I know how he made you feel. Sage, I know he hasn't been around for long. But you were different when he was in your life. A good different. These past few weeks, I've seen a more vivacious, more dedicated, happier woman than I've ever seen. Don't let that go just because you're scared now."

"I'm not scared, Harper. I'm being realistic." Monticello jumps on the couch, and I stroke the cat, thinking about everything that's danced in my head for days. Thinking about all the missed calls and knocks at the door I've ignored.

"Realistic? Since when are you realistic? Think about Evermore. Everyone told you to be realistic, and what did you do? You went full charge, said screw the doubters, and look what you've built. You've never prided yourself on a cautious life. Why are you changing your ways now? Why are you afraid to give it a chance?"

"With him in Texas? Harper, he's a player. So am I, quite frankly. Do you really think we're going to be able to stay committed, to make it work, with so much distance between us?"

"What's the alternative? To cry yourself into a coma in your condo and then pretend like none of it happened? It seems to me like you don't have a choice but to give it a try, really."

I sigh. How would it work? This is new territory, something I don't want to face.

"I'm fine, Harper. I don't need him. I'm fine without him."

I stand and head to the kitchen to get some coffee.

"Now let's talk about the design plans for the next launch," I say, shoving all thoughts of Cash aside. I've had my fun, entertained the idea that my heart could settle down. But that's over now. I'll be fine without Cash or love or any of those other stupid sentiments everyone thought I needed.

I'll be fine on my own, just like I've always been.

At least that's what I tell myself as I work away the day and climb into the cold sheets at night, praying that sleep will come quickly and that the tears will fade with time.

THIRTY-TWO

Cash

———

"ABOUT DAMN TIME YOU SHOW UP. HONESTLY, THIS NEW generation. Do any of you know the first thing about work ethic?"

The man rubs his graying moustache as he hobbles inside the door of his apartment, holding open the door just wide enough for me to sideways scramble into the place he calls home. His face seems permanently frozen in a scowl. I carry my sad excuse for a toolbox, hoping I can remember the steps that Levi had walked me through over the phone.

"And don't you think for a second I'm leaving you alone. I've got plenty of valuables in here, so don't get any ideas." The man practically barks the words at me as he shoos me towards the back room where the broken washer rests. I inhale. This is going to be a long, long, long afternoon.

Thank goodness I'll be going back to Texas, away from this phony career and miserable life here. Thank goodness I've regained my wits and haven't let my heart dictate my future. Right?

I shove down the pangs of guilt and heartbreak that have been keeping me up at night. I shove aside the image of Sage's smiling face, the thought of her body moving under mine in perfect harmony—

"Well, boy, hop to it. I don't have all damn day to watch you fart around."

Back to reality it is.

I sit down, reminding myself to stay calm and confident. I am a brilliant lawyer who passed the bar. I can handle a messed-up hose in a washer, can't I? I try to walk back through Levi's instructions. Why hadn't he just come over and taken care of it? That's what he should have done. In a few weeks, he'd have to take care of it, anyway.

I set to work removing the cover, listening to Mr. Crenshaw bark orders and complain and swear at my incompetence.

And that's when it happens. The water sprays everywhere when I loosen the hose much too quickly, getting Mr. Crenshaw soaking wet. I sit there, confused about what to do next, and convinced that it's all just hopeless. Hopeless indeed.

"Don't worry, brother. We can't all be expert handymen like me," Levi teases as we head back to my office after he came in and saved the day with Mr. Crenshaw. The washer was mercifully fixed, and all is right again.

Except my pride.

"That man's a nightmare. How do you deal with him?" I ask. The cantankerous renter apparently had been living in the apartment since Grandad first bought the place.

"Well, I feel sorry for him, actually," Levi murmurs as we walked into the office.

"Why?"

"Grandad said he's lived alone all those years. Never married. No kids. Just all alone. I think it's made him sort of grumpy."

I look at Levi to see him giving me a matter-of-fact look.

I exhale loudly, heading to the window. "Go ahead. Say it, brother."

"Say what?"

"You think I'm being a fool." My hands are in my pockets. I stare out over the lawn of the apartment building, looking into the vast ocean view in the distance.

"Hey, I didn't say it."

"You don't have to," I respond, turning to look at my brother's know-it-all face.

"Well, if you don't need someone to say it, then it must mean you already know it's true."

"What am I supposed to do, Levi? Give up my career, my life in Texas for a girl I just met? Who is a player? What if it doesn't work out?"

Levi grins, readjusting his hat. I think about chucking it out the window, I hate it so much.

"Here's the thing about that question, Cash. There's always another side. Because what if it does?"

What if it does. It's a thought I've been tossing around since Sage stormed out of the Coffee Hole, since I realized exactly how she felt and what she was thinking. Not that I'd admit that to Levi.

But love is complicated. It's why I've always avoided it. And two players can never really play for keeps, can they? Not with distance and different careers and doubts between them.

I was always meant to go back to Texas. This was never permanent. I was never meant to settle down.

These are the mantras I chant to myself as I head back to my place for the night, thinking about how empty the bed is without her—and wondering if I'm making the biggest damn mistake of my life. Wondering how it will feel to go back to my bachelor pad in Texas, alone with booze, women, and a broken heart bigger than Texas.

THIRTY-THREE

Sage

I SLING BACK THE SECOND MARGARITA, MY EYES glancing about for the prey I'm looking for. There's a guy in the corner, a redhead who has an Ed Sheeran vibe if I squint a little bit. But a brunette comes slinking up to him and kisses his cheek. Dammit. Taken.

I peruse the dance floor, looking for a lonely guy on the outskirts. I come up blank. I see a blond at the bar wink at me, but he's wearing an outfit that screams country and also not my type. His boyish face says he's a boy who plays for keeps, not just to play. Been there done that. I need something else tonight.

I sashay around the Marooned Pirate wearing my sexiest dress, desperately needing to get back on my game. I need a good lay to get Cash Creed off the mind. I need to go back to the Sage Everling I was at the beginning of summer, before he ruined my whole game. I need to go back to the love him and leave him mentality that has served me well all these years.

But that's the thing about opening your heart up. It's hard to close it back up again.

I find a corner booth, and a few men come over and offer to buy me a drink. One is too short and one is too arrogant and one is just not my type. None of them stir any sort of attraction in me, not even the one-night kind of attraction. I sit in the booth, sucking down another margarita, realizing it's all for naught. I'm ruined. I'm destroyed. I'm never going to play well again.

Because, as I finish my final drink and head out of the bar, I realize the hard truth.

I can't play the game because none of them will be Cash. I'll never find another one like him. And beneath my player's heart, the truth rings.

I don't want to play the game anymore unless it's with him.

A woman on a mission—and I don't back down from a mission—I stomp towards the curb, order an Uber, and realize what I have to do.

It's not too late. I can still play—and win. I can win this game after all.

Sage

I'VE NEVER BEEN THIS NERVOUS. *FOCUS, SAGE,* I TELL myself. *Get your A-game on. You're confident and sexy, and you've got this in the bag.* But even the margarita in my hand and Levi's help last night isn't making me very reassured. I'm out of my element. This isn't my typical game.

But it's too late to back out because when I look up, he's walking through the door. Just like last time, the whole crew is with him. Levi's ushering him in. I notice his face is a little sullen, and he's not as confident as last time. He looks like he's been forced to come here. It's okay, though. I can work with this. He's here, that's what's important. And even if I lose this round, I've got to try. I've just got to try.

So I do the thing I never imagined I would do. I

strut up to the man who I want to claim as mine, who I can see forever with. I walk up to a man with more than a one-night stand in mind. I walk up to him with the hopes of not seducing him, but of winning him back. It's a risk, but one I have to take.

He's wearing some nice designer jeans and a button-up shirt, just like last time. But there's stubble on him, the kind that he wears well. Just like the first time I saw him, his look screams business professional, and there's still that familiar touch of arrogance I've come to appreciate as reserved confidence. He's scoping the place out, and he glances over at me, staring for a little bit longer than a friendly appraisal. His eyes study mine, and this time there's no doubting it.

He sees me. He wants me. He's interested.

I give him a coy smile as I sip my margarita. He's here to play, and so am I. But it's a different kind of play this time, one we're not completely familiar with but will learn to be.

I fluff my hair strategically, tossing my head to the side as I walk over as confidently as possible, my stilettos leading the way. Cash doesn't take his eyes off me. It feels good.

I amble up to the tall, handsome stranger and say, "Hi, I'm Sage. Can I buy you a drink?" There's a pause, and I wonder if maybe it's not going to work out like I thought. But that stoic face turns into a full-on grin.

"Cash Creed. And how about we do things the other way around? What are you drinking?"

I smile confidently up at him, his eyes making my heart flutter in the familiar way I've come to love. "Mr. Creed, that's not how I do things. I don't need any man to take care of me."

"Is that so?" he asks.

"I can take care of myself. So how about I buy you a drink, you tell me all about yourself, and then you ask me to dance?"

"Forward much?" he asks, teasing me with his eyes. I get a whiff of his cologne, and it's the one that drives me crazy.

"Always. Life's too short for anything else."

"Jack and Coke, then," he says, and I smile, brushing past him to flag down the bartender.

I get his drink and we find our way to a table.

"So," I begin as he says, "Listen." I shake my head.

We're really much better at being forward.

"Cash, here's the thing. When you first walked into this bar, I was a player without a mission. I was determined to keep my walls up and to protect my heart. I didn't think I needed to let anyone in. And then you came along. Everything changed."

"I feel the same way," he murmured, kissing my cheek. "And I'm sorry. I should've realized that things have changed. It's just... it got so complicated so fast. I didn't plan on falling in love. I didn't think when I made plans to return to Texas that I was going to meet you, that you were going to change everything. And now I've got a career and you, and you're in two different states."

I shush him, putting a finger to his lips. "I know. And I have a career and you, too. The thing is, I don't want you going back to Texas and us having to do long distance. But I also don't want you giving your career up for me. That won't do either."

Cash exhales. "What then?"

I grin. "I've always thought I'd look pretty sexy in a cowboy hat, if you want to know the truth. And I could use a change of scenery for some fashion inspiration."

Cash raises an eyebrow. "What are you saying?"

"My career is great because it lets me go anywhere. I can design for Evermore anywhere, and with technology, I can work with my employees from anywhere, even Texas. But I can't have hot, nightly sex with you when we're hundreds of miles apart. I can't see where this relationship goes or continue feeling so damn happy with you in my bed if we're miles apart."

"I was hoping you would say that."

"Then, Mr. Creed, I have a proposition."

"I like propositions."

"I hope you like this one. How about we skip the one-night stand tonight. How about we do a string of one-night stands? The kind that you move in together for?"

Cash leans over and takes my jaw in his hands. He kisses me, warm and hard, a sensuous kiss I've been missing.

"I think that sounds perfect."

"But it is against your rules," I tease, winking at him.

"Maybe it's time we reinvented them, then," he says as he pulls me out of the booth and to the middle of the dance floor, where we dance like the first night we met.

Epilogue

CASH

Two months later

Her fingers wrap around mine as we prepare for takeoff, the next stop home. In truth though, I'm already home in more ways than I can imagine, the beautiful woman beside me making everything just feel right.

"So you really think your mama's going to like me?" she asks, leaning her head on my shoulder.

"Darling, she's been calling me every few hours to make sure it's for real and that you're really coming with me."

"Well, I can't blame her. Look at you. Hard to believe someone would willingly settle down with Woodville's biggest playboy."

"Yeah, well, Mama doesn't know that I've settled for Ocean City's biggest playgirl. Guess there are some things just better left in the dark."

Once we're in the air, we both look out Sage's window, studying the clouds. "I still can't believe you're coming with me."

"You better not be regretting it. Because you're stuck with me now," she replies, and I lean in to kiss her cheek.

"No regrets here. But what about you? I still feel sort of bad you're uprooting everything."

She smiles. "I think it's going to be an amazing adventure. A new boutique in Texas, bringing Evermore to an actual brick and mortar store. These are the things of my dreams, Cash. And more importantly, I get to do it with you."

When Sage decided she wanted to move back home with me, I'd called in a few favors with some friends in real estate back home. I had the perfect storefront in mind for Evermore, and they made it happen. We've got a lot of work to do in order to get Evermore up and running, but it's going to be perfect. Sage is going to take Texas fashion by storm, and I can't wait.

She snuggles into me, and I lean on her head, thinking about how much things have changed.

Thinking about how I headed to Ocean City not knowing who I was, not realizing what I was missing. And now I'm coming back with a whole new adventure ahead of me and a fiancée that makes me crazy in all the right ways.

"So I fully expect you to give me the entire Texan tour when we get there. I need to see this place, to experience it in its entirety. I have no doubt you can pull that off."

She pulls back to look at me, giving me a wink. I kiss her on the cheek. "Don't worry, I've already been thinking of tons of places to explore with you. In all sorts of ways."

She raises an eyebrow. "And how are the women of Woodville going to take this? The most eligible bachelor off the market officially?" she asks, holding up her left hand, the diamond I put on it last month sparkling. When we play, we go all in, apparently. At least we do now that we're playing a new game.

I shrug. "Well, it's no secret there were a lot of... shall we say conquests? They might be a little upset. Who can blame them, really?" I tease. I love that we're both open about who we were and that there's no judgement.

Sage's eyes sparkle. "Well, I'm not worried.

Because I conquered the unconquerable in love, so I'm feeling pretty good about my ranking."

I shake my head. "Unbelievable," I say, teasing her with my eyes.

"What?"

"Well, Miss Everling, I just think you've got it all wrong. I'm pretty sure I was the one who conquered you."

"Don't you wish," she says, leaning back against me, shaking her head.

I smile, resting back in the seat as we head off to our new life, the conquered and the conqueror.

And no matter which way the truth is, no matter who is in what role, I think the bottom line is this. We've both learned that lone hearts are overrated. This feeling, this connection right here, is what real life is all about.

Acknowledgments

First and foremost, I want to thank all of the beautiful readers of the Lines in the Sand series for following these characters and embracing all of their quirks. I have really enjoyed spending time with the Midsummer Nights' crew, and I'm just so thankful that all of you have picked up their books.

Thanks to my amazing publisher, Hot Tree Publishing. Becky, you forever changed my writing career when you welcomed me into the Hot Tree family. I'm so blessed to call Hot Tree home to all of my romances and am so thankful to work with such an amazing team. Thank you especially to Olivia and the entire editing team who helped me get the story ready for the world.

I want to thank my parents, Ken and Lori, for

supporting my dreams and teaching me to love reading at a young age. Thank you to all of my friends and family who have been along for the ride on this entire adventure. Thank you to my amazing husband for always cheering me on, for being right beside me at all of my events, and for believing in my dreams.

And last but not least, thank you to my best friend, Henry, for always being up for a good cuddle on the couch with cupcakes when I need to just relax.

An English teacher, a romance author, and a fan of anything pink and/or glittery, Lindsay's the English teacher cliché; she loves cats, reading, Shakespeare, and Poe.

Lindsay's goal with her writing is to show the power of love and the beauty of life while also instilling a true sense of realism in her work. Some reviewers have noted that her books are not the "typical romance." With her novels coming from a place of honesty, Lindsay examines the difficult questions, looks at the tough emotions, and paints the pictures that are sometimes difficult to look at. She wants her fiction to resonate with readers as candid, poetic, and powerful.

Inked Hearts, released in 2017 with Hot Tree Publishing, was named a Romance Times Top Pick. Additionally, Remember When, released in April of 2017, was named a Route One Reads Romance Pick by the Pennsylvania Center for the Book.

Lindsay currently lives in her hometown of Hollidaysburg, Pennsylvania, with her husband, Chad (her junior high sweetheart); their cats, Arya, Amelia, Alice, Marjorie, and Tyrion; and their Mastiff, Henry. In addition to being a huge bookworm, Lindsay's also a fan of cruelty-free makeup, coffee, chocolate, Netflix, and shopping.

Website: http://www.lindsaydetwiler.com

Goodreads: https://www.goodreads.com/author/show/13508159.Lindsay_Detwiler

Newsletter sign up: http://www.tinyletter.com/lindsaydetwiler

About the Publisher

Hot Tree Publishing opened its doors in 2015 with an aspiration to bring quality fiction to the world of readers. With the initial focus on romance and a wide spread of romance subgenres, Hot Tree Publishing has since opened their first imprint, Tangled Tree Publishing, specializing in crime, mystery, suspense, and thriller.

Firmly seated in the industry as a leading editing provider to independent authors and small publishing houses, Hot Tree Publishing is the sister company to Hot Tree Editing, founded in 2012. Having established in-house editing and promotions, plus having a well-respected market presence, Hot Tree Publishing endeavors to be a leader in bringing quality stories to the world of readers.

Interested in discovering more amazing reads brought to you by Hot Tree Publishing? Head over to the website for information:

www.hottreepublishing.com

More From Hot Tree Publishing

Want more great romances? Check out Hot Tree Publishing's collection of mixed-genre romantic reads.

Amy McClung

Ann Grech

Avery Sterling

Carolyn LaRoche

Charyse Allan

Dahlia Donovan

Eva King

Gen Ryan

Genevive Chamblee

Heidi Renee Mason

Jas T. Ward

Jackson Kane

Jane Matisse

Kolleen Fraser

Krissy V

Laura N. Andrews

Lindsay Detwiler

Mary Billiter

Megan Lowe

ML Nystrom

MV Ellis

Natalina Reis

Samatha Harris

Sidney Valentine

Skye McNeil

Theresa Oliver

Virginia Cantrell

www.ingramcontent.com/pod-product-compliance
Lightning Source LLC
Chambersburg PA
CBHW032107180726
48284CB00002B/483